getting it

ALEX SANCHEZ

Simon Pulse
New York London Toronto Sydney

This book is a work of fiction. Any references to historical events, real people, or real locales are used fictitiously. Other names, characters, places, and incidents are the product of the author's imagination, and any resemblance to actual events or locales or persons, living or dead, is entirely coincidental.

◆

SIMON PULSE
An imprint of Simon & Schuster Children's Publishing Division
1230 Avenue of the Americas, New York, NY 10020
Copyright © 2006 by Alex Sanchez
All rights reserved, including the right of reproduction in whole or in part in any form.
SIMON PULSE and colophon are registered trademarks of Simon & Schuster, Inc.
Also available in a Simon & Schuster Books for Young Readers hardcover edition.
Designed by Steve Kennedy
The text of this book was set in New Caledonia.
A glossary of Spanish words appears on page 211.
Manufactured in the United States of America
First Simon Pulse edition October 2007
10 9 8 7 6 5 4 3 2 1
The Library of Congress has cataloged the hardcover edition as follows:
Sanchez, Alex.
Getting it / Alex Sanchez. —1st ed.
p. cm.
Summary: Hoping to impress a sexy female classmate, fifteen-year-old Carlos secretly hires gay student Sal to give him an image makeover, in exchange for Carlos's help in forming a Gay-Straight Alliance at their Texas high school.
ISBN-13: 978-1-4169-0896-8 (hc)
ISBN-10: 1-4169-0896-X (hc)
[1. Coming of age—Fiction. 2. Homosexuality—Fiction. 3. Friendship—Fiction.
4. Mexican-Americans—Fiction. 5. High schools—Fiction. 6. Schools—Fiction.] I. Title.
PZ7.S19475Ge 2006
[Fic]—dc22
2005029905
ISBN-13: 978-1-4169-0898-2 (pbk)
ISBN-10: 1-4169-0898-6 (pbk)

Also by Alex Sanchez

Rainbow Boys
Rainbow High
Rainbow Road

So Hard to Say

The God Box

To first love

Acknowledgments

With gratitude to my editor, David Gale; my agent, Miriam Altshuler; associate editor Alexandra Cooper; and all those who contributed to the creation of this book with their encouragement and feedback, including Bruce Aufhammer, David Bissette, Bill Brockschmidt, Kevin Case, Jeremy Coleman, Erik Ekman, Mariel Fox, Bill Hitz, James Howe, Chuck Jones, Jingjo Kongmun, Erica Lazaro, Kevin Lewis, Mark Lyons and Joe Scavetta, P. J. McCarthy, Sara McGhee, John Porter, John "J. Q." Quiñones, Phoom, Bob Ripperger, Kara Skubel, Kelly Stewart, St. Andrew's High School, Pattawish Thitithanapak, Tim Vance, Mike Walker, Scott Wiggerman, and the McCallum High School GSA. Thank you all.

One

FIFTEEN AND STILL a virgin, Carlos Amoroso wanted more than anything to get a girlfriend—and hopefully get laid.

Yet he broke into a sweat and lost his breath anytime he went near a girl. Like now: He was carrying his tray across Lone Star High's crowded cafeteria, peering out from beneath the frayed hood of his sweatshirt. Ahead of him, a group of golden-skinned beauties garnished their hot dogs at the condiments counter, chatting and giggling.

In the center of the pack stood Roxana Rodriguez. With each laugh, her clingy top inched up her bare slim midriff above hip-hugging jeans. Long, shading lashes fanned her jade-green eyes. Thick eyebrows arched like the wings of an angel. Above her ruby lips rose the graceful nose of an Aztec princess. And long, blonde-streaked hair curtained across her shoulders toward her mesmerizing boobs. She was the girl Carlos yearned for.

For her part, however, Roxy didn't seem to even notice Carlos— and since starting high school the previous year he'd yet to summon the nerve to utter a single word to her. But in his secret dreams, the JV cheerleader swarmed all over him.

"I totally want you," she panted, making such crazy love to him that his heart nearly burst.

The day after such reveries he usually slinked past her, his head down, a little hung over with embarrassment. But in last night's dream, the vision of her tearing his pants away had seemed so real it had startled him awake. And he'd resolved that today he'd give her his screen name.

During morning classes, he'd turned the folded note over in his damp fingers, rehearsing what he'd do: He'd stride straight up to her, jut his chin out, and say, "'S'up? Here's my screen name. IM me."

Simple. Clear. Confident. Except . . . First, he glanced over at his lunch table to make sure his friends weren't watching. Then he took a deep breath and jostled his tray through the cafeteria crowd toward the sophomore girls.

"He's not getting into my pants," a girl in a leopard-print top said, "but I might get into his."

"I know." Roxy extended her hot dog across the condiment counter, one chrome-studded-jean hip thrust out. "Guys can get so needy when you start dating them."

Carlos wasn't sure what Roxy meant. He knew she wasn't dating anyone. He'd asked around. Everyone confirmed Roxy was single. He put his trembling tray down.

But Roxy failed to notice him as she stroked the ketchup pump, protesting with a sly smile to her friends: "I can't get it to squirt."

Alongside her, a girl with cherry-red lipstick burst into giggles. "If anybody can, you can."

"Yeah," Leopard Girl agreed. "Try talking dirty to it."

Carlos recognized his chance to be Roxy's hero, though he didn't want to become the butt of the girls' joke.

Too late. Roxy's eyes latched onto him, as if he really was her hero. "You're a guy. Show us how you do it!"

The other girls darted conspiring glances at one another, grinning and giggling.

"Um . . . sure . . . um . . ." Carlos wrapped his fingers around the pump nozzle. "You just—"

"Mmm, muscles!" Roxy squeezed her fingers around Carlos's

biceps, shooting bright, unexpected heat arrows up his arm. The blood raced in his arteries. Sweat burst from his pores. His body quivered. And a spurt of ketchup shot out sideways from the unclogged pump, striking the front of his jeans. *Splat!*

"Oh, my God!" The girls exploded into peals of laughter.

"You must do that a lot," remarked Leopard Girl.

"I'm surprised he hasn't gone blind," squealed Lipstick Chick.

"Nice technique." Roxy smiled as she ketchuped her hot dog. Then the group strode away, laughing and whispering.

Carlos's heart crumpled like the folded note still inside his sweatshirt pocket. Not only had he failed to give Roxy his screen name, he'd made a complete fool of himself. How would he ever get her to like him?

But at least she'd talked to him. And with that encouraging thought, he lowered his tray to cover the splotch on his crotch and headed toward his friends' table.

Two

As Carlos approached his buddies' table, Playboy's eyes flashed at the red ketchup stain. "Dude, what happened? You get your period?"

Beside him, Pulga snorted so hard that Coke exploded out his nose. "You forget your tampons?"

"For that you'd better get a super-size Kotex," Toro chimed in.

"Shut up." Carlos plopped his tray down, secretly reveling in the attention.

The group had been his friends since boyhood, beginning with flea-size Pulga. He'd latched onto Carlos in kindergarten, newly arrived from Veracruz, not speaking a word of English. Carlos translated in whispers to him, and in turn, Pulga rewarded him with what seemed like the world's funniest booger jokes.

In second grade, Toro joined their class. Eager to make friends, he showed Carlos and Pulga how to pitch softballs, shoot baskets, and kick field goals. His athletic prowess, strong, thick build, and calf-brown eyes quickly prompted his nickname, Spanish for "bull."

Later that year, Playboy transferred to their school, sporting a self-possessed confidence that drew the boys like a magnet. His slick black hair, handsome looks, and wide-set eyes gave him an air of utter scorn. On a dare from Pulga one day, he brought his stepdad's *Playboy* to show-and-tell, and his nickname was born.

"You going to walk around like that?" Playboy now tossed Carlos a wad of napkins to dab the ketchup stain.

"You'd better put some water on it." Pulga handed Carlos a cup of ice water.

"Uh-oh," Toro remarked as Carlos dripped water onto the crotch spot. "Now you look like you peed yourself."

"So how'd you get Roxy to talk to your sorry ass?" Playboy asked, obviously impressed.

"Yeah." Toro leaned forward. "Why was she squeezing your muscle?"

Pulga snickered. "I'd give her a different muscle to squeeze."

Carlos's buds knew all about his crush on Roxy. He never stopped gushing about her. And though he now gave them a modest shrug, inside he glowed with pride.

"She wants you, man," Toro said, punching Carlos's shoulder.

"Yeah." Pulga chuckled as Carlos wiped his crotch, making a wet red smear that totally looked like he'd gotten a period. "She wants you to use a tampon."

"What you need is backup," Playboy advised, laying an arm around Carlos's shoulders. "I'll help you with her."

Playboy boasted the most experience with girls, having been the first of them to lose his virginity—with a senior girl he'd met on a teen website. He'd gloated to the group how she'd been so hot for him she'd yanked out a condom and ordered him to put it on. Since that first time, Playboy had become practically a pro at web hookups— though Carlos was never clear as to exactly what constituted a hookup. Sometimes Playboy described it as just making out; other times he claimed going total. Whichever the case, it was more than Carlos was getting.

"Thanks, but no thanks." Carlos slid out from beneath Playboy's arm. He trusted Playboy with almost everything—except Roxy.

"Why don't you hook up with someone easier?" Pulga suggested. He'd become devirginized six months earlier with Carlotta Romero, the tallest girl in sophomore class (nearly a foot taller than Pulga).

Since then, he got an afternoon matinee once a week when her mom volunteered with the homeless. Yet Pulga insisted Carlotta wasn't his girlfriend. "She's just a friend"—he grinned wryly—"with benefits."

"What you need," Toro now told Carlos, "is to get laid."

Toro claimed to have lost his virgin status last summer with a girl from another school named Leticia, though he was sketchy about details. That left only Carlos as a definite virgin. In fact, he'd never even mouth-kissed a girl.

"Duh!" Carlos slouched down in his cafeteria chair. "I *know* I need to get laid."

"Find a babe from another school," Playboy suggested. "If you screw someone from here, the whole school will know. Don't shit where you eat. That's my motto." He gave a loud, punctuating burp.

Carlos gazed from beneath his olive-green hood across the lunchroom at Roxy. Couldn't his friends understand he wanted more than a hookup? He wanted a girlfriend: someone he could talk to and do stuff with, who would listen and not make fun of him; someone he could count on. In his dreams, that girl was Roxy. Plus, she was incredibly hot.

"I'll go talk to her for you," Toro volunteered.

At least Carlos trusted Toro more than Playboy. But Toro had the jock muscles Carlos lacked. What if Roxy liked him better? Besides . . . "That's, like, so elementary school."

"Well," Pulga scolded, "high school isn't the place for anything serious. Wait till you're thirty and no one hot wants you anymore."

No one hot wants me now, Carlos thought.

When the bell rang, Playboy suggested, "Wrap your sweatshirt around your waist or everyone's going to laugh at you."

"I've got some shorts in my locker you can change into," Toro offered.

"Uh-oh," Pulga warned Carlos, "he's trying to get you out of your pants."

"Shut up." Toro swung at him, but Pulga ducked away.

As the boys carried their trays to the return line, they found themselves alongside Salvador "Sal" Encarnación, a senior who everybody said was gay—though that didn't mean it was true. He was a tall, thin guy, about the same build as Carlos, with spiky brown hair and shiny little hoop earrings in both ears.

"Watch your backsides," Playboy cautioned his group.

"Screw you!" Sal shot back.

"Yeah, you'd like that," Pulga snickered.

Carlos had never understood why guys harped so much on the gay thing. But even though he felt sorry for Sal, he didn't stop his friends. He knew that if he spoke up, his buds would give him endless crap too, like "Woo-hoo, Carlos has a boyfriend!"

Instead, he turned away, watching Roxy strut out of the lunchroom and feeling a little less like a hero than he had before.

Three

THAT AFTERNOON, CARLOS followed his English class to the school library to choose a book to report on. He selected *The Virgin Suicides*—a story he thought he'd relate to.

While waiting to return to class, he noticed a table full of girls whispering and laughing softly about starting some club. Among them was Pulga's benefit-friend, Carlotta, who waved to him. Beside her, a girl wearing an orange hoodie also smiled at him. And sitting with the girls was Sal, the alleged gay guy.

As Carlos began to read his book, he occasionally noticed how relaxed and comfortable Sal seemed with the girls, displaying none of that guy show-off-ness that Carlos's buds got into around chicks. How come? Was Sal really gay? How could he be, with all those girls practically swarming over him? Maybe that was the real reason guys called him queer: They were jealous.

On the bus ride home after school, Playboy returned his attention to Carlos's lunchtime ketchup incident: "How's your flow?"

Pulga and Toro laughed like a couple of delighted hyenas.

"Shut up," Carlos told them. "You bunch of *pendejos*."

"Pendejo" was the boys' favorite put-down for each other. Literally, it meant a pubic hair, though in Mexican slang it was like saying "moron" or "dumb ass."

Playboy gloated about a girl from another school he was hooking up with that afternoon.

As though not to be outdone, Pulga announced, "I've got my matinee with Carlotta."

And Toro followed suit, as if not to be left out: "I wish Leticia lived closer—or that I had a car. She e-mailed me saying she's crazy-horny for me."

Carlos sat up in his seat. "Would you guys shut it?"

"What's your problem?" Playboy asked.

Pulga smirked. "He's just stressed 'cause he ain't getting any."

Toro gave Carlos a sympathetic nod. "I know how you feel, man."

As soon as Carlos got to his apartment, he unrolled the ketchup-stained jeans from his backpack, brought them to his nose, took a deep breath, and thought, *For the rest of my life, whenever I smell ketchup I'll think of Roxy.*

Then he gazed into the mirror—not exactly his favorite pastime. He pulled his sweatshirt hood down and ticked through his mental checklist of things he didn't like about himself:

BODY PARTS THAT ARE FREAKISHLY BIG

Nose	☑
Ears	☑
Elbows	☑

PARTS THAT ARE PATHETICALLY SMALL

Arms	☑
Chest	☑
Scrotum	☑

He thought his eyebrows looked like fat caterpillars, while his face was a pimple party. His brown hair hung like an unruly mop, and his teeth seemed more dingy than white. And yet . . .

He pulled off his sweatshirt, rolled up his shirtsleeve, and flexed his arm. A small lump—barely tennis-ball size—swelled in his biceps. Could it truly have impressed Roxy?

Yeah, right. No wonder the girls had laughed.

He tugged his soft, well-worn hoodie back on and went to the kitchen for a Coke, chips, and cheese curls. Then he phoned his pa, a construction foreman, at his cell number.

"Hey, *mi'jo!*" his pa answered.

In the background, Carlos could hear the banging hammers, beeping equipment, and shouting voices at the construction site.

"How were the girls today?" his pa asked. Ever since Carlos had begun grade school, his pa had always asked about the girls, like he expected Carlos to be some big Casanova.

"The girls were good," Carlos replied proudly, eager to tell him how Roxy had spoken to him and squeezed his arm. Maybe his pa could give him some advice.

"Today I talked to—"

His pa interrupted. "I bet they're good! God, I wish I were your age again. Those were the best years of my life."

"Uh-huh." Carlos tried to continue. "Today I talked to this girl named—"

"Hold on a sec." His pa cut him off again. Carlos listened as a man yelled something and his pa shouted back. Then he returned to Carlos: "Look, *mi'jo*, I'm a little busy now. See you Saturday. *Te quiero.*" He hung up as Carlos whispered, "Love you too."

A familiar ache stirred in his chest. He wished he could talk more with his pa, but ever since the divorce three years ago he only got to see him once a week. Even then he had to share him with the beautiful young secretary his pa had left his ma for, and their toddler son.

Carlos tossed the receiver onto its cradle. What good would it do, anyway, to get advice about girls from a man who'd thrown away his marriage?

Carlos waded across the bedroom carpet, past discarded candy bar wrappers, strewn clothes, and video game cartridges to his computer. After pulling out his homework assignments, he put on his head-phones, cranked a Tejano mix full blast, and returned his thoughts to Roxy.

Four

CARLOS EKED OUT his homework in between thinking about Roxy and IM-ing friends, till his ma arrived home.

"You're lucky to have a mom so pretty," people always commented. Carlos agreed that she was beautiful, with her cinnamon-colored eyes and slim figure—although she seemed so short since he'd spurted past her in the last year.

"'S'up?" he now greeted her, prying his headphones off.

From the bedroom doorway, she scanned the chaos of his room and gave a smile of resignation. "*Mi amor,* how can you work in this mess?"

Carlos shrugged. At least once a week his ma hassled him to clean his room, but she never actually made him do it. Since the divorce, she'd pretty much stopped making him do anything.

She pulled the pins from her hair so it cascaded over her shoulders. "How was school today?"

Although Roxy remained foremost on Carlos's mind, he felt uneasy telling his ma about her. In contrast to his friends and his pa, who shared guy horniness about females, it felt too weird to think of his own ma feeling anything like that.

"Um, school was fine, except I need your help with math."

Fortunately, his ma worked as the accountant for an auto parts chain. "Let's go over it after dinner. Remember, Raúl is coming over."

Raúl was her boyfriend—actually her third since the divorce—a tall, brawny car mechanic, nothing like Carlos's short, skinny pa.

Twice a week he came over for dinner, bringing dessert, after which he watched TV with Carlos's ma and stayed the night.

Tonight he brought over flan, a favorite of both Carlos and his ma. After dinner, his ma helped Carlos with his geometry, sitting close beside him at the dining table.

Carlos recalled how when he was a boy his ma would drape her arm around him, stroking her fingertips through his hair as she cradled his head into the warm soft cushion of her chest. But since starting high school it made him feel weird to sit so close to her, and he now scooted his chair away.

After they finished with his math, Carlos returned to IM-ing his friends, playing computer games, and thinking about Roxy. Around nine thirty, his ma knocked on the door to say good night. "Don't stay up too late, okay?"

She kissed him on the back of the neck and Raúl waved. "Sleep well."

Carlos waved back. He liked Raúl, except for one thing: Even though his ma closed her bedroom door, Carlos could still hear the faint squeak of bedsprings as she and Raúl went at it. It was a little gross. No, it was *truly* gross. Carlos didn't want to think about his ma getting it on, especially with someone she wasn't even married to. But how could he tell her that? Besides, he knew how hurt she'd been by the divorce. He wanted her to be happy. So, he put his headphones on and cranked up the volume.

Around ten thirty, he went to finish up the flan and watch TV. First he turned on an episode of *Cops* where they busted some toothless eighty-six-year-old who'd hooked up with a thirteen-year-old girl. Then he switched to a reality show in which eight college guys and girls shared a house, fighting all day but secretly boning each other at night. Was there *any* program that wouldn't remind Carlos he was the only person on the planet not getting laid?

Last he clicked on *Queer Eye,* a show where five gay dudes gave some grungy straight guy a makeover—plucking his nose hairs, redecorating his apartment, and teaching him to bake a quiche—so he could confidently propose marriage to his girlfriend and she'd tell him "yes." Which, of course, she did. On TV, the guy always gets the girl.

As Carlos watched, he recalled Sal, the supposedly gay guy at school. It was then that the idea first popped into his brain: If Sal truly were queer . . . Could he possibly help Carlos? . . . Not to propose to Roxy, of course—at least not yet—but to get her to maybe like him?

Immediately, he chucked the thought. This was real life, not some dumb TV show. Roxy wasn't his girlfriend. And Sal wasn't some makeover star.

Around eleven o'clock, Carlos gave a huge yawn, shut the TV off, and ambled toward his bedroom. After pulling off his sweatshirt, he peered in the mirror again. Squinting, he blurred his vision as though underwater and tried to imagine himself as handsome and confident.

No luck. Maybe after a super-size makeover. Dismayed by the reflection staring back at him, he draped his sweatshirt over the mirror. Then he kicked aside a plastic soda bottle, stripped to his briefs, and climbed beneath the tangle of bedcovers. But he couldn't stop thinking about that crazy idea.

Five

ON SATURDAY MORNING, while Carlos scrounged through piles of clothes for a clean shirt, he thought again about asking for Sal's help, but once again discarded the idea.

A little after noon, his pa picked him up for their weekend visit, along with his wife, Lupita, and their toddler son, Henry.

Carlos had first met Lupita when he was little, at his pa's construction office. His pa had often taken him to job sites to show him off, propping a hard hat on Carlos that nearly slid over his eyes. Lupita, the site office secretary, had smiled and taught Carlos how to volley jellybeans and catch them in his mouth. Not until she got pregnant did Carlos realize she and his pa had been having an affair.

Then Carlos felt painfully torn. He overheard his parents' arguments and watched his ma cry, yet he didn't want his pa to leave. The divorce had been wildly confusing. Carlos resolved that his own relationship with a girl would be different—committed and faithful.

In the meantime, like now at McDonald's, he politely tried to once again like Lupita. But how could he? She'd broken up his family.

He also tried to like his little half brother, but he missed having his pa to himself. To make matters worse, today Henry pooped in his diaper, making an awful smell.

After lunch the four of them drove to the city park. When Carlos was a boy, his pa used to help him catch all types of insects in jars and nets, taught him to preserve them in lighter fluid, and showed him how to carefully pin them to Styrofoam without breaking them apart.

Carlos had amassed an awesome collection of butterflies, bees, grasshoppers, and, his prize possession, a female praying mantis.

After the divorce, the bug collection had gotten lost piece by piece in the ever-mounting mess of Carlos's room. He now felt too old to chase insects. Instead, he scratched a stick among the initials and dates on a wood bench and wished he could go back in time, as he watched his pa and Lupita push Henry on the merry-go-round.

In the middle of the playground, amid the brown-skinned Mexican families, Carlos noticed a pair of white adult guys with an Asian toddler girl.

"I think they're *maricones*," his pa muttered as he sat beside Carlos on the bench.

His pa's Spanish word for "queer" made Carlos recall Sal and the wild idea of asking for his help with Roxy. Maybe he should ask his pa what he thought.

"Do you, um, know anyone who's gay?"

"No." His pa crossed his arms, giving Carlos a sidelong glance. "Why would I?"

His pa often got macho that way—like the time his ma had tried to teach Carlos how to resew a loose button on a shirt, causing his pa to protest, "You trying to turn him into a girl?"

Recalling that, Carlos decided best not to mention Sal. Nonetheless, the makeover idea kept worming its way through his brain.

Six

AS THE WEEKEND progressed, Carlos began pondering: If he were to approach Sal, how could he do so without anybody seeing him? After all, probably part of the reason Sal always hung with girls was because no guy wanted to be caught talking to him—at least no *straight* guy.

At school on Monday, Carlos began tracking Sal's moves, piecing together his schedule. Sal's bold-colored shirts—magenta, turquoise, pink—and shiny hoop earrings made him easy to follow down hallways. Every so often, Carlos thought he saw Sal glance over his shoulder and spot him, but Carlos quickly ducked away. By week's end, he had Sal's schedule down pat, but he still couldn't pick out a good time or place to talk without someone seeing him.

He noticed, however, that after last period Sal walked home alone. As Carlos's bus drove past, he watched Sal turn down a side street only three blocks away from school.

The following day, when the final bell rang, Carlos told his friends he was staying after school.

"What for?" Playboy asked, his eyebrows arched in curiosity.

"I've got to do something." Carlos gave an evasive shrug. "That's all."

"Like what?" Pulga extended a bag of caramel popcorn toward Carlos, as if bribing him to tell them.

"Um, nothing." Carlos took some popcorn and tried looking away, but his three friends had surrounded him. "Just something for school."

"Is it some sort of secret?" Toro dug into Pulga's bag of popcorn.

"No, it's just—it's not important."

"Then what is it?" Playboy insisted with a burp.

"Nothing, I told you!" Carlos shifted his feet, worried he'd lose Sal. "You're going to miss your bus."

His buds exchanged confused glances, then Playboy said, "Dude, you're really getting weird," before the three of them headed toward their bus.

Quickly, Carlos hustled in the opposite direction and out the main door, blending into the students walking home.

He easily trailed Sal's bright lime-colored shirt. Sal seemed to glance over his shoulder once, but Carlos quickly hid his head inside his hoodie and waited for Sal to turn the corner. Once off the main street, Carlos reasoned, they could talk without anyone from school seeing.

When Sal turned onto the side street, disappearing behind a tall hedge, Carlos made his move. He sprinted to catch up, but when he turned the corner, Sal was nowhere in sight.

Carlos stopped and caught his breath. He gazed down the empty street of quiet houses and parked cars. Where could Sal have gone?

Behind him, the bushes rustled. As Carlos turned, Sal slammed into him, tackling him at the waist. Carlos sprawled onto the grass, the breath knocked out of him.

Next thing Carlos knew, he was flipped over, his pack jabbing into his back, his arms pinned to the ground. Sal sat astride his chest, shouting, "Tell me why you're following me!"

"Let me go!" Carlos gasped, struggling to push Sal off.

But Sal pressed down harder on his arms. "Tell me!"

Pain seared through Carlos's wrists as he strained to get free. "Get off!"

"No!" Sal refused to loosen his grip. "Not till you tell me!"

Carlos gazed up at Sal, confused by the situation. If Sal were gay, why wasn't he acting weak and girly? What if he *wasn't* gay? Clearly, Sal could beat the *caca* out of him.

Carlos stopped struggling. "I wanted to ask you something," he muttered.

"Ask what?" Sal clamped down harder on Carlos's wrists.

Carlos groaned. In light of the circumstances, did he dare ask? "Are you really, um . . ." He hesitated before squeaking out, "gay?"

Sal stared at Carlos, frowned, and loosened his grip, rolling off Carlos. "Oh, God! Not *another* one."

Carlos took a huge breath as Sal's weight left his chest. He quickly sat up and peered over at Sal. "Not another what?"

Sal propped himself up, then stood, dusting off his jeans. "Another so-called straight guy who wants a blow job. You're the third one this year. I'm not interested, okay? So leave me alone."

"Huh?" Carlos scrambled to his feet, pulling his hood onto his head. "That's not what I want!"

Sal perched his hands on his hips and gazed at him dead-on. "Then what do you care if I'm gay or not?"

Carlos shifted his feet. Now that he actually stood face-to-face with Sal, the whole makeover idea seemed not only crazy, but embarrassingly stupid. Yet, given what Sal had thought Carlos wanted, he felt he had to explain himself. "It's just, um, I wanted to ask . . . if you could, um"—he cleared his throat—"help me?"

Sal gave him a long, steady look. Then his brow softened. "Look, dude," he said gently. "If you think you're gay, you probably are. I can't tell you if you are or not. Join the Gay-Straight Alliance we're starting. That'll help you figure it out. In the meantime, try visiting some porn sites—gay ones and straight ones. Whichever turns you on more, that's probably what you are. Okay?"

"No!" Carlos protested. "That's not it! I *know* I'm straight."

Sal threw his hands in the air. "Then what the hell do you want?"

Carlos answered slowly, trying to make his shaky voice sound confident. "Um, I want you to help me with, um . . . a girl . . . you know, to get her to like me."

Sal gave Carlos a sideways stare, till finally he asked, "Are you for real? You're straight? And you want *me*—a gay guy—to help you get a girl?"

"Yeah." Carlos shoved his hands into his pockets, feeling foolish.

Sal rubbed his chin as if doubting. "And you're *straight*?"

"Yes!" Carlos felt like saying, *Forget it!* Instead he said, "You know, like on that show *Queer Guy*."

"You mean *Queer Eye*?" Sal corrected. "Okay, let's say you are straight. And I should help you *because* . . . ?"

Carlos realized he'd never stopped to consider that. "Um, I guess . . . because . . . I need your help."

"Right." Sal smirked. "Just like you helped me last week in the cafeteria when your asshole friends gave me shit."

Carlos gazed down at the ground. He didn't like Sal calling his buds assholes. "They didn't mean anything by it. They're good guys. They just act like that sometimes."

"Oh, yeah?" Sal said. "Well, let me ask you something: Why should a girl like you when you just stand by, watching your friends act like jerks, and even defend them for it? Because you know what? That makes you a jerk too."

Carlos stared down at his shoes. Sal was right: Why would any girl like him?

Out of the corner of his eye, he watched Sal turn away down the sidewalk. Then Carlos looked up and shouted, *"Please?"* He felt pathetic saying it, but if Sal didn't help him, who would?

As if reconsidering, Sal stopped in front of a ranch-style house and looked back at Carlos. But then he waved his arms, shooing him away. "I told you, no!" He climbed the front steps and disappeared into the house, slamming the door.

Carlos waited several minutes, hoping Sal would come back out. Then he turned toward home. As he trudged the twenty blocks, squinting into the afternoon sun, he pondered his bleak life ahead, wondering: Was he destined to be a girlfriend-less virgin forever?

Seven

THE FOLLOWING DAY at lunch, Playboy bragged about some girl who'd shown him her boobs on web-cam. But the blurry, depth-distorted photo on his cell phone made the breasts look more like a pair of pancakes.

"Hey," Pulga commented with a burp, "that looks like my breakfast."

"I wish I'd had her for breakfast," Toro chimed in.

Abruptly, another boy's voice intervened: "Okay, I'll do it."

Carlos sat up, stiff as a Popsicle. Sal loomed over their table, staring directly at him.

"On three conditions," Sal continued. "First . . ." He held up his index finger. "You tell your creep friends here not to give me shit—ever again."

Carlos felt his throat going dry. Didn't Sal realize this was supposed to be a secret?

"Second . . ." Sal added another finger. "It'll cost you six bucks an hour plus expenses. Believe me, I'm letting you off cheap. Start by bringing twenty bucks tomorrow. And most important"—Sal flicked out a third finger—"you help start our school's Gay-Straight Alliance."

With the word "gay" all eyes turned to Carlos. He cringed, wanting to crawl beneath the lunch table.

"Now for your first lesson." Sal dabbed a finger across the corner of his own lips. "When you're eating, wipe your mouth."

Embarrassed, Carlos quickly swabbed his mouth with his sweatshirt sleeve, smearing a mustard-yellow line across the olive green.

"Dude, not with your sleeve!" Sal groaned and spun around, shaking his head as he walked away.

When Carlos glanced back at his buds, their eyes were all trained on him.

"What's up with that?" Playboy's face scrunched up as if he'd eaten something sour.

"What're you paying him for?" Pulga scowled.

Toro leaned forward, whispering, "Are you friends with him?"

"N-n-no . . ." Carlos felt like a chicken bone had caught in his throat. "I just, um, asked him to help me with something."

His three buds exchanged suspicious glances. "With what?" Pulga asked. "Getting BJs?"

"Shut up." Carlos stared down at his tray.

"Dude . . ." Playboy sounded concerned. "You're not turning queer on us, are you?"

"Fags are gross," Pulga remarked, but then added, "although lesbians are cool."

"I'm not turning queer." Carlos crossed his arms.

Toro asked, "Then how come you're going to help start that gay club?"

"I'm not!" Carlos shot back.

"*Pendejo,*" Playboy said solemnly, "you're holding out about something."

For the first time, Carlos saw the hurt in his friends' eyes, and he couldn't blame them. The four of them had always known every secret about one another, no matter how personal: how Carlos's pa had ditched his ma for a younger woman; how Playboy had gotten crabs from a hookup last summer—and how he had to shave all his body hair to get rid of them; how Pulga had secretly tied a condom to the principal's retractable car antenna so it flapped in the breeze as he pulled in and out of the faculty parking lot for three days before he noticed; how Toro had gotten noticeable wood during a wrestling match. How much more personal could you get?

Yet, this was different. How could Carlos explain that, when it came to girls, he felt like a hopeless loser compared to them?

"Look, I asked him to help me with a project, that's all. I'll tell you about it later. In the meantime, leave him alone, okay?"

His three friends looked at one another. No one said any more about the incident. When the boys boarded their bus that afternoon, Sal seemed forgotten. But on the ride home, Playboy sat farther away from Carlos than usual. Pulga didn't make any of his usual wisecracks about women in passing cars. And even when they pulled beside a convertible, allowing them to see straight down a woman's sizable cleavage, none of them went the remotest bit crazy.

Eight

As Carlos walked home from the bus stop, about a billion questions bounced around in his brain. Should he tell his friends the truth about his makeover idea? What if they laughed at him? Why had Sal changed his mind? Was he planning to try something funny? He'd better not; Carlos only wanted his help to get a girl, nothing more. Also, what had Sal meant by expenses? And one more thing: What the hell was a Gay-Straight Alliance, anyway?

Upon getting home, Carlos grabbed some corn chips, cookies, and root beer. Then, out of curiosity, he did a web search on Gay-Straight Alliances—GSAs.

He spent over an hour reading about them. Apparently, they truly weren't gay clubs. They were supposed to "build understanding between straight and gay students" and "help address homophobic name-calling." The groups sounded interesting, but when Carlos woke for school the following morning, he still couldn't decide whether to actually agree to Sal's terms.

Nevertheless, he searched for bills and coins beneath the piles of crap on his desk and dresser. Somehow, he managed to scrape together twenty bucks.

When the lunch bell rang, Carlos waited in the water fountain alcove outside the cafeteria, pulling his hood low over his brow so no one would recognize him, and pretended to get a drink. When he spotted Sal, Carlos signaled him.

"Um, here." Carlos quickly shoved a fistful of coins and crumpled bills into Sal's hands.

"Don't you have a wallet?" Sal asked, unfolding each bill.

"Um, I don't really need one." Usually, the only things Carlos carried in his pocket were his lunch card and school ID.

"Well, get one anyway," Sal ordered. "You want girls to think you're poor? Wait, on second thought, I'd better help you pick one out. Let's get started this afternoon. I'll take the bus with you."

A lump knotted in Carlos's throat. Sal ride the bus home with him? What would his friends say? What would the others on the bus say?

"Wa-wa-wait," Carlos stammered.

"What?" Sal raised an eyebrow as though reading Carlos's thoughts.

Carlos bit into his lip. "Um, never mind."

Sal gave a shrug. "Meet you after school." He stepped toward the cafeteria, sliding Carlos's bills into his wallet.

Carlos slumped against the hallway wall, not the least bit hungry, and wondering, *What have I gotten myself into?*

To complicate matters, Playboy invited the group to go over to his house after school—to help him create a profile for one of those teen websites where guys and girls could post photos and hopefully hook up.

During afternoon classes, Carlos tried to think of a way out of his dilemma, with no success. After the last bell he shuffled reluctantly toward the main door. From behind him, someone yanked his sweatshirt hood off his head.

"Hey, *pendejo!*" Playboy swung an arm around Carlos's shoulder as they stepped outside into the sun. Alongside him were Toro and Pulga. "Did you come up with some ideas for my profile?"

"Um . . ." Carlos slowed his steps as he approached their bus. "Why don't we do it tomorrow? So I have more time to think."

"I can't tomorrow," Toro said. "I've got wrestling practice."

"Come on, boys!" The bus driver revved the motor, signaling she was about to leave.

Carlos let his friends board ahead of him and glanced over his shoulder. Sal was nowhere in sight. Maybe—hopefully—he'd forgotten. Or perhaps agreeing to help Carlos had only been a ruse to get twenty bucks. If so, it was a small price to pay for chucking the whole wacky idea.

But just as Carlos was about to climb aboard the bus, a voice called behind him, "Hey! Sorry I took so long."

Carlos's heart plummeted. Quickly, he suggested to Sal, "Um, why don't we just walk?"

"How far do you live?" Sal asked.

Carlos shifted his feet. "Not far."

"How far?" Sal insisted.

"Um . . ." Carlos scratched his neck. "About twenty blocks."

"Screw that!" Sal stepped onto the bus.

Carlos watched from the sidewalk, debating. Maybe he should let the bus leave without him—or just wait till it started moving and accidentally throw himself in front of it.

The driver revved the motor again. "You coming or aren't you?"

Carlos heaved a sigh and climbed on board as the bus began its bumpy ride.

Nine

"SIT HERE!" CARLOS told Sal, grabbing the first empty bus seats—as far away as possible from his back-row buds. Unfortunately, that meant sitting beside Vicky Vasquez, a girl Carlos had been friends with till middle school, when she began dressing weird—in porkpie hats, polka-dot stockings, and other uncool stuff that made people start to call her "Freaky Vicky the Lesbi."

Carlos didn't know what dressing weird had to do with being a lesbian. Yet, out of concern for his own rep, he began avoiding her, reasoning that she'd brought the stigma upon herself.

"Hi, Vicky!" Sal now called out.

"Hi, Sal," she yelled across Carlos, ignoring him as he peeled off his backpack. "What are you doing on this bus?"

"Going to Carlos's," Sal shouted back.

Carlos slunk down in his seat. Did Sal have to announce the fact loud enough for the entire bus to hear?

"Be careful," Vicky warned Sal, darting a scornful glance at Carlos. "He'll turn on you."

Carlos cringed, wishing he could disappear. Not only had he ditched his friends and had the school queer inform the entire bus he was going to Carlos's, now Vicky had reminded everyone she used to be his friend. Carlos's entire high school rep seemed to be careening out of control.

The instant the bus reached his stop, Carlos whispered to Sal, "Come on!"

"Hey!" Vicky called after him. "You forgot your backpack."

Carlos grabbed it and hurried out the door. As the bus pulled away, he peered from beneath his sweatshirt hood toward the rear window. His buds' faces stared back at him, brows furrowed in confusion.

"Why are you so stuck-up?" Sal asked as they walked toward Carlos's white-stucco apartment complex.

"I'm not stuck-up," Carlos muttered, shoving his fists into his hoodie pockets.

"Yeah, you are," Sal insisted. "You didn't even say thanks to Vicky for handing you your backpack."

"She's a freak." Carlos defended himself. "Just look at how weird she dresses. No one talks to her."

"Dude, it's called being an individual. That makes her a freak?"

Carlos kept silent, uncertain how to respond. On *Queer Eye* they hadn't told the straight guy to talk to some freakazoid lesbian. As Sal and he crossed the parking lot toward his building, a panicked thought crossed Carlos's mind: Was Sal planning to turn him into a freak?

Ten

CARLOS SWUNG OPEN his apartment door and stepped inside. But Sal remained standing outside, scowling as if Carlos had just farted in his face.

"Um, what's the matter?" Carlos asked.

"Dude . . ." Sal gave a sigh. "When you're with someone, don't just barge ahead of them. Open the door and let them go first."

Carlos flushed warm from embarrassment—and annoyance. "*Dude*," he echoed sarcastically, "you're not a girl."

"Doesn't matter," Sal shot back. "It shows you're considerate—or *not*."

Carlos narrowed his eyes, debating whether to tell Sal, *Go blow yourself!* Grudgingly, he stepped back out to the corridor and stood aside.

"Thanks." Sal strode past him into the living room.

"You're welcome," Carlos grumbled, silently adding, *pendejo*.

As Carlos closed the front door, the phone began to ring. He jogged to get it, but upon seeing Playboy's number displayed on the caller ID, he stopped short and let the call roll to voicemail.

"You want something to eat?" he asked Sal.

Inside the kitchen, he tossed packs of snack cakes, corn chips, and marshmallows onto the kitchen table. "Grab whatever you want, man."

Sal stared at the pile. "Have you ever read the ingredient labels for this junk? It's all fat and sugar."

"So?" Carlos ripped open a snack cake, stuffing it in his mouth. "It tastes good."

"Yeah, and it does nothing to help your skin."

Carlos winced and stopped chewing, embarrassed by his pimples. "For real?" He couldn't help notice Sal's skin—not completely unblemished but definitely clearer than his own.

"Haven't you got anything more healthy to eat?" Sal replied. "Like fruit or something?"

Carlos's ma constantly nagged him to eat more fruit, but she'd never suggested it might be better for his skin. He opened the fridge and grabbed a couple of apples, tossing one to Sal. Then he pulled out a two-liter bottle of Coke.

"You should lay off that, too," Sal told him. "It's total sugar and stains your teeth."

Carlos clamped his lips together, hiding his teeth and feeling even crappier about himself. Wasn't a makeover supposed to make him feel better?

"Just water for me," Sal told him as Carlos downed a glass of Coke.

Before Sal could get a chance to pick on something else, Carlos led him toward his room, remembering to stand aside, muttering, "Ladies first."

"Whoa!" Sal stopped in the doorway, scanning the chaos. "Did a bomb explode in here? And why do you keep it so dark? It's like a cave." He stepped in, kicking aside a soccer ball as he drew open the window blinds.

The second-story bedroom looked out over the apartment complex playground, where Carlos's pa used to play with him when he was little. Now Carlos usually kept the blinds down.

Sal turned back toward the room. "How can you live like this? You must feel like a mess."

"I don't feel like a mess," Carlos argued, though it did frustrate him every time he couldn't find a schoolbook or clean shirt.

"And what's that awful smell?" Sal waded across the room, poking the toe of his shoe at heaps of DVDs and video games—till he bent over a dirty clothes pile and unearthed Carlos's favorite pair of sneakers—a gift from his pa. Although they were frayed and no longer fit, Carlos had kept them, unmindful of their smell. Till now.

"I should've worn a biohazard suit." Sal fanned a hand in front of his nose. "You do wear socks, right?"

"Um . . . ," Carlos mumbled.

Sal rolled his eyes. "No wonder these stink. You've got to wear socks—clean ones, *every* time."

Carlos burped—the effect of the Coke.

"Hey!" Sal shot him a look. "I know this may shock you, but no one wants to hear your bodily functions. Now, can you get us some plastic bags?"

As Sal turned away, plucking clothes off the floor, Carlos secretly sneered at him. Then he went to get some bags from the kitchen, wondering, *What's cleaning up my room got to do with getting a girl-friend?* But he recalled the queer guys on TV redecorating the straight dude's apartment. And even Carlos's friends called his room a pigsty.

In short order, Sal had helped Carlos to stuff two huge bags full of skanky clothes and carry them downstairs to the laundry room.

"You wash whites in hot water to make them whiter," Sal explained, "and colors in cold so they don't fade."

Carlos's ma had told him that, but he was usually too lazy to sort his clothes. "What difference does it make?"

"Because," Sal explained, "girls notice how bright or dingy something is, even if guys don't."

Back in Carlos's room, they sorted through mountains of crap, hauled dirty plates to the dishwasher, and organized his school stuff. In between, Carlos asked about something he'd been wondering: "So, like, um, what do you think made you gay?"

Sal popped a DVD into its case. "What do you think made you *straight*?"

Carlos shrugged. "I was born that way."

Sal snapped the DVD case shut. "And I was born this way."

Carlos pondered that. As furniture emerged from beneath the debris, Sal commented, "It's looking better. But the place needs some drama. Something uniquely you."

"Huh?" Carlos wondered: what the hell Sal was talking about? Then, from beneath a pile of board games, Sal uncovered Carlos's collection of butterflies, bees, and beetles pinned to Styrofoam.

"You collect *bugs*?" Sal's face twisted in disgust. "Well, I guess it makes sense with you living like this."

He started to toss the Styrofoam panel into the trash bag, but Carlos grabbed it away from him. "No! Don't throw those out!"

Sal's brow crinkled in surprise.

"My pa helped me collect them," Carlos explained.

Sal's glance shifted between Carlos and the bugs. "Well . . . ," he said at last, "then I guess they're something uniquely you. Set them aside for now."

Carlos carefully propped the panel of bugs against the wall. Then they went to put the clothes in the dryer. As they returned from the laundry room, Carlos asked Sal something else he'd been wondering: "Do your parents know you're gay?"

"Are you kidding?" Sal laughed. "They figured it out before I did. That's why I'm so well-adjusted."

Carlos didn't get what Sal meant. It seemed like every time he asked Sal a question, the response was never what he expected.

Amid a final pile of stuff, Sal discovered Carlos's female praying mantis. "Whoa! Now *this* is drama." He gazed admiringly at the shiny green insect. "Hey, aren't these the bugs that eat their boyfriends after getting it on?"

"Yeah, sometimes," Carlos replied, though he'd never thought of their mates as boyfriends.

"Well, we'll definitely have to do something with this." Sal gently laid the mantis aside and looked at his watch. "But for now, we'd better finish."

Carlos saw the time and frowned. Nearly three hours had passed. How long would this take? The TV show only lasted an hour for the entire makeover. And yet, he felt guilty complaining; no one had ever helped him pick up all his crap before.

Sal helped him lug six garbage bags to the Dumpster, fold and put away his clean laundry, make the bed, and even vacuum the carpet.

"We'll figure out what to do with the room next time," Sal said, grabbing his backpack to go. "Anything special you had in mind?"

"Um . . ." Carlos gazed around the tidied room, recalling the TV guys redecorating the straight dude's apartment. "Um, I always wanted a headboard. You know, like people on TV have. But my ma says they're too expensive."

"Hmn." Sal peered at him. "Let me think about it, but I'll need another twenty bucks."

Carlos bristled, not knowing where he'd get the money. But he said, "Okay."

He was sitting at his computer when his ma came home. She gazed around his room wide-eyed and grabbed the doorframe, pretending to steady herself from shock. "*Mi'jo! ¿Qué pasó?* Your room looks great!"

She whisked across the clean carpet and gave him a big, long hug that smashed his nose. He took advantage of her exuberance to ask, "Can I have twenty bucks?"

Her arms fell away from his shoulders as she gave him a curious smile. "Oh, I get it. So that's what this is about. What do you need twenty bucks for?"

Carlos shrugged. "To fix up my room some more."

His ma's face scrunched up. "What do you want to do with it?"

"I don't know."

When he went to sleep that night, he still wasn't sure how cleaning up and redoing his room was going to help him get Roxy. But at least his ma had given him the money. And he did feel better about himself—so long as he didn't think about having to face his buds the next day.

Eleven

THE FOLLOWING MORNING, Carlos woke as soon as his alarm sounded. His head felt unusually clear as he gazed around his newly organized room. After showering, he put on a clean shirt, underwear, and socks, feeling like a new man. But as he walked toward his bus stop, he filled with dread. Now he had to face his friends, whom he'd ditched the day before.

"'S'up?" Carlos greeted them as he climbed into the back row.

The boys gazed silently at him till Playboy finally spoke: "So, did you hook up with your butt-monkey?"

"Shut up. I told you, he's helping me with something."

"Lending you a hand?" Pulga made a jacking-off gesture.

"Did he try anything funny?" Toro asked.

"Would you guys grow up?" Carlos snapped. Fortunately, they shut up.

In between second and third period, Carlos shuffled down the hallway. Turning the corner, he stopped cold. Roxy was marching straight in his direction, her strut seamless and carefree. Her beautiful boobs bounced beneath her tight red top, in sync with the clip of her shiny black boots, as she talked and giggled with her friends.

"Who has time for a boyfriend?" one girl was saying.

"I know," Roxy replied. "Between cheerleading, choreography class, and chorus, I barely have time to breathe."

In his freshly laundered clothes, Carlos felt braver than he'd ever felt near her. Quickly, he pulled the folded notepaper with his screen name from his sweatshirt pocket, his breath quickening as the girls approached. Summoning all his nerve, he stretched out his hand toward her, holding the notepaper. "'S'up, Roxy? Here's my screen . . ."

But Roxy didn't even turn her head. Her eyes remained focused on her girl friends, as they sauntered past.

Carlos's heart crumpled like the paper he shoved back into his pocket. *I may as well not even exist,* he thought, pulling his sweatshirt hood low over his forehead.

When the lunch bell rang, he waited for Sal at the water fountain alcove. "Here!" He handed Sal the twenty his ma had given him. "How long is this going to take?"

"I don't know." Sal casually inserted the twenty into his wallet. "As long as necessary. I've got to get some stuff for your room. I'll let you know how much it costs."

"Huh?" Did he think Carlos was made of money? "What kind of stuff?"

"I haven't decided yet." Sal turned toward the lunchroom. "I'll go with you tomorrow afternoon."

"Wait!" Carlos shuffled his feet, recalling the previous day's experience with his buds and Freaky Vicky. "I don't want to take the bus."

Sal turned to stare at him. "Why? You scared to be seen with me?"

"No," Carlos lied. "It's just . . . I don't want everyone at school finding out what I'm doing."

Sal's gaze softened slightly. "Okay. Then I'll come over Saturday."

"But, um . . ." Carlos shuffled his feet some more. "That's my day with my pa. How about Sunday?"

"Nope," Sal replied. "Can't do Sunday. I'm in choir at church. After that I hang out with my boyfriend."

Boyfriend? Had Sal really said "boyfriend"? Carlos glanced over his shoulder, desperate to end this conversation *fast.*

"So," Sal went on, "it's either after school or Saturday. Take your pick. Hurry up, I want to eat lunch."

"Okay. How about Saturday morning?" His pa wouldn't come over till noon.

"All right." Sal nodded. "I'll be over at eight."

"*Eight?*" Carlos groaned. He usually slept till eleven on weekends. But before he could say any more, Sal had slipped away.

Twelve

AT LEAST WITH Sal coming over on Saturday, Carlos was able to avoid his friends' finding out. He also forgot to tell his ma. Saturday morning she woke him, nudging his arm. "Carlitos, a boy named Sal is here. He brought a can of paint—and some bamboo. What's this about?"

Carlos's brain slowly cleared from sleep as his eyes blinked open. "Um . . ." He sat up, rubbing his face. He felt too embarrassed to tell her the full extent of his plan with Sal, so he simply said, "Remember I told you I was going to fix up my room?"

His ma gazed around the bedroom. It was getting messy again, with video games and dirty clothes piling up on the floor.

"So, is it okay to paint?" Carlos asked, even though he wasn't sure what they'd paint.

His ma glanced up at the posters of megababes in bikinis that lined his wall. It only took a second for her to reply, "Sure."

Carlos pulled some clothes on, stopped by the bathroom, and headed to the kitchen. His ma sat at the breakfast table with Sal, sipping coffee. She was laughing—not something she usually did with his friends. In fact, she didn't really laugh much at all since the divorce.

"'S'up?" Carlos told Sal and grabbed some Sugar Puffs from the cupboard. Sal glanced at the cereal box and slid the sugar bowl across the table to Carlos. "Why don't you just spoon out the sugar bowl for breakfast?"

"That's what I've told him!" Carlos's ma nodded agreement. "He had two cavities his last checkup."

"Ma . . ." Carlos frowned. "That was three years ago."

"That long?" she replied, just as the doorbell rang. "I'll have to make you another appointment."

She left the boys to tend to a client for her home sewing business, and Sal commented, "Your mom's pretty. You've got her eyes, you know that? They're, like, honey-colored—really nice."

As Sal gazed at him, Carlos chomped on his Sugar Puffs. No one except his ma had ever told him he had nice eyes before. Sal better not be planning to try anything funny.

Carlos quickly wolfed down his cereal, eager to forget Sal's compliment and get to work. He helped Sal carry the gallon of paint, brushes, some bamboo stalks, and a Plexiglas box-frame to the bedroom.

"Hey!" Sal shouted at the sight of the unmade bed and crap accumulating on Carlos's floor. "I didn't spend all that time helping you clean up just for you to slob the place up again. It only takes fifteen minutes a day to keep it neat, okay? That includes making the bed. A messy bed means a messy head."

Carlos clenched his jaw. He didn't like being chewed out. But how could he argue? Besides, Sal was already making the bed. "Get the other side," he ordered Carlos. In fifteen minutes, the room was tidy again.

"Now, first we're going to paint an accent wall," Sal announced.

"Huh? What's that?"

"It's when you paint one wall a different color. I got auburn to go with the beige carpet. Tell me you don't hate auburn."

Carlos didn't know what the hell auburn was, but glanced at the color on the paint can. "It looks okay. But how come we're only painting one wall? Won't that look weird, like we ran out of paint?"

"No. It'll look stylish." Sal scanned the walls, focusing his gaze on the big-boobed babes. "Hey, you haven't told me: Who's the girl you're so hot for?"

Carlos bit the inside of his lip, hesitating. What if Sal revealed to Roxy what they were doing? Carlos would surely be the laughing stock of school. "Um, I'd rather not say."

Sal stared at Carlos, his brown eyes clouding. "Then I guess I'm out of here." In an instant, he'd gathered the paint supplies and bamboo, heading toward the door.

"Hey, wait!" Carlos blocked his path. "What . . . ? Why do you need to know who she is?"

"I don't." Sal glared at him. "But if we're going to do this, you've got to trust me."

Carlos took a breath. Could he really trust Sal? Only Carlos's closest friends knew about his crush on Roxy. Slowly, he let out his breath. "Promise you won't tell her what we're doing?"

Sal's brow arched in confusion. "Why would I tell her?"

"I don't know." Carlos shrugged, feeling foolish for being so paranoid. "It's, um . . ." He cleared his throat. "Roxy Rodriguez."

"Roxy?" Sal's voice rose in surprise. "Are you serious?" He gave a wild laugh. "Dude! She's, like, totally not your type."

Carlos cringed, edging back. Did Sal think Roxy was out of his league? Or that Carlos wasn't good enough? That he was a loser? He suddenly didn't like Sal at all. "You don't know my type!"

"Oh, come on!" Sal retorted. "Roxy is, like, Miss Plastic—with all that makeup she wears? Her eyes aren't even really green. Those are contacts. And those crotch-high skirts? She's, like, totally wrong for you."

Carlos tried to remain calm, but inside he felt ready to blow a gasket. Makeovers weren't supposed to work this way. The TV queer guys never tried to talk the straight guy out of liking the girl—nor made her sound like a slut.

"What do you know about girls?" Carlos shot back. "You're a fag!"

Sal winced, his face hardening. "Whoa, man. Stop right there. Number one, I don't like being called fag, or 'homo,' or 'perv,' or anything else besides gay. Number two, whether I'm gay or not, I just think . . ." His face softened with concern, his eyes gentle with compassion. "You deserve better than her."

Yeah, right, Carlos thought. Any guy at school would give his left nut for Roxy—any straight guy. "I want to ask you something." Carlos stared defiantly back at Sal. "Why are you really doing this—helping me?"

"I told you," Sal said, his voice unwavering. "So you'll help with our GSA."

But Carlos sensed there was more to it. He waited, arms crossed, till Sal came forth: "You're right. There's another reason. All through school, almost every straight guy I've known has called me 'fag' and treated me like shit. I'm curious to see: Are you really any different?"

Carlos glanced away, confused. *Was* he different from other straight guys? In what way? Was he "turning queer," like Playboy had said?

Carlos squared his shoulders. "I'm not gay, if that's what you're thinking."

Sal rolled his eyes. "I think your room has proven that!" He gave a gentle sigh. "Look, I'm sorry I said Roxy was plastic. If you like her, you like her. And it's none of my business. I was out of line, okay? I agreed to help you and I will. But don't call me names, all right?"

Carlos wished he hadn't called Sal a fag. It made him uneasy the way Sal now looked at him—trusting and tender—like his ma sometimes looked at him after he'd messed up and felt sorry.

"Do you think I'm a loser?" Carlos blurted out, without even thinking. "My friends think I'm a loser for not just hooking up with someone and getting it over with."

"*It?*" Sal's eyebrows rose up. "Getting *what* over with?"

"You know—getting laid."

Sal peered at him. "Is that what this is about? I thought you wanted a girlfriend."

"Well, I do, but—" Carlos plopped down on the bed, his thoughts spinning. "I get confused. Sometimes I don't know what I want."

"Maybe. . . ." Sal shrugged. "That's because life isn't about what you *get*, it's about what you *give*."

Carlos peered up, not exactly sure what Sal meant. After all, you didn't *give* laid, you get laid. And you *get* a girlfriend.

"Look," Sal said softly, "you're not a loser. A slob maybe, but not a loser." He cracked a smile. "If you want a girlfriend, then I think you should have one. Just don't settle for less, okay?"

Nobody had ever talked to Carlos this way. He really didn't know what to make of Sal, but he suddenly liked him more than ever. "Okay."

Sal glanced at his watch. "Let's get to work."

Carlos happily returned to the project at hand. He asked his ma for an old sheet to use as a drop cloth and the boys painted an "accent wall" surrounding the window.

When they'd finished, Sal announced, "Next comes your faux headboard. 'Faux' means 'false.' Let's move your bed out."

They painted an auburn rectangle onto the wall behind the bed. Carlos liked how the color matched the window wall. And it did look like a headboard, like he'd always wanted.

Next, Sal returned his attention to the bikinied babes. "Can we please take down those posters?"

Carlos blushed, but he didn't want to take down the girls. They'd become almost real, doing all sorts of cool stuff with him inside his brain.

"Come on," Sal coaxed. "I'm sure you've got plenty of other photos on your computer."

Carlos turned even redder. Grudgingly, he pried out the pushpins and rolled up the babes, carefully storing them in his closet. Meanwhile, Sal delicately arranged Carlos's praying mantis in the Plexiglas box-frame he'd brought. Then he centered a hook above the painted headboard and nailed it up.

Framed on the wall, the bright green insect no longer looked like some kid's bug, but like a masterpiece of art. Next, Sal put the bamboo stalks in a metal can and stood them in the corner. The place truly looked like something the TV guys would've done.

"How did you learn to do all this stuff?" Carlos asked.

"I don't know . . ." Sal hesitated. "I guess maybe growing up gay you spend more time by yourself. Hardly anyone wants to be your friend. None of the guys will come near you—and you try to figure out why. So you notice things—how people dress, wear their hair, decorate their room . . ." Sal shrugged. "Maybe that's how I learned it."

Carlos tried to imagine what it would've been like to grow up without his buds. He felt kind of sorry for Sal.

"Here are the receipts for the paint and display box," Sal said as the boys cleaned up the paint stuff. "I already had the roller and pan, so no charge for those. I cut the bamboo from my yard."

Carlos stared at the receipts, totaling more than eighteen dollars. How did Sal expect him to keep getting so much money? "I'll have to give you the money next time. Do you think we'll finish by then?"

"I doubt it. Next we've got to tackle your clothes. You'll need to get some more money."

Oh, great, Carlos thought. *Money from where?*

As they crossed the living room, Sal waved. "Good-bye, Mrs. Amoroso."

"Bye!" She glanced up from her sewing and gave him a big smile. "Come back anytime!"

Carlos didn't get why females were so charmed by gay guys, but he was glad his ma liked Sal. And as he returned to his room to pack his overnight bag for his pa's, he found himself kind of wishing he could've spent more time with Sal.

Thirteen

As usual, Carlos's pa arrived late. And, as always, he cell-phoned from the parking lot, to avoid coming upstairs. It annoyed Carlos how his pa and ma had gotten so weird about each other.

Carlos said good-bye to his ma and carried his overnight bag down to the car. Lupita sat in front arguing with his pa about Henry's binky bottle. Henry was strapped into a kid seat in back, crying. Carlos climbed in beside him and put his music player headphones on.

Like every Saturday, they drove to McDonald's. Over lunch, Carlos told his pa and Lupita, "A friend helped me paint an accent wall in my room."

"What's an accent wall?" his pa asked.

It surprised Carlos that his pa, a construction foreman, didn't know. "It's when you paint one wall a different color."

His pa raised an eyebrow. "Only one wall?"

"That sounds pretty," Lupita commented, and fed Henry a French fry.

"It looks cool," Carlos said. "Then we painted a headboard onto the wall."

"That's clever!" Lupita beamed.

His pa frowned. "Where did your mother get the money for a headboard?"

"She *didn't*," Carlos muttered. "I said, my friend and I *painted* it on."

Carlos didn't say any more after that, not mentioning the framed praying mantis or the bamboo stalks.

After lunch, they went to the park, where his pa and Lupita played with Henry. Carlos sat on a bench, bored, and wondered why he'd even bothered to come along.

After the park, they went to the mall to buy new clothes and shoes for Henry.

"He's growing so fast!" Lupita exclaimed, fitting Henry into a new pair of pants.

"Yeah, too fast," his pa griped.

"I need some new stuff too," Carlos told his pa. "Can I have some money?"

His pa pressed his lips together, unsmiling. "Look, *mi'jo,* at the rate Henry is going through clothes, I can't right now. Why don't you ask your ma? I already sent her the check for this month."

Carlos turned away from his pa, his face burning. He understood Henry needed clothes, but what about *him*? "I'm going to the car," he announced and walked out.

On the way home, they stopped for a DVD rental. Carlos wanted an action movie, but instead his pa got a crappy "family" film that Henry could watch.

For the rest of the evening, Carlos kept to himself, bored out of his mind. When it came time to sleep, he lay restless on the bed beside Henry's crib. The nightlight illuminated the gazillion brightly colored toys that filled Henry's room. It wasn't fair that Henry should get so much stuff while Carlos couldn't even get some clothes money.

Next morning, he slept late and woke up feeling too cranky to say much.

His pa watched him warily. When he dropped Carlos off at home, he handed him a ten-dollar bill. "Here. I'm sorry it can't be more."

Wow, ten whole dollars? Carlos thought sarcastically. *Big whoop.* But he took the money anyway.

When he got to his room, he went to his computer, eager to catch up with his friends and take his mind off his turdy life.

Fourteen

CARLOS KNEW his friends were still pissed at him for not telling them what was going on with Sal. Although they'd stopped hassling Sal, they still gave Carlos crap, telling him, "Hey, there goes your Hoover," or, "I think you're starting to lithp."

Although the comments irritated Carlos, he also felt a little guilty for not being honest about what he was doing. Sunday afternoon he invited the group over to hang out. When they reached his bedroom doorway, the boys gazed in awe around the clean, redecorated room.

"Holy crap!" Playboy gasped. "What happened?"

"I decided to fix it up."

"How come you painted only one wall?" Pulga asked. "You run out of paint?"

"It looks cool," Toro said. "Can you help me paint my room like this?"

"Sure." Carlos smiled. "That's called an accent wall, to match the faux headboard."

His three friends stared at him as if he were an alien.

As the boys hung out, the discussion turned to Playboy and the Internet profile he'd set up—which so far hadn't turned out so good. He'd placed it on Hot-or-Snot.com, a teen hookup site where your photo could be rated on a scale of one to ten by anyone who saw it. Anything over five meant you were hot. But under five, you may as well crawl beneath a rock and die.

Since Playboy had posted his photo/profile, his rating had slipped steadily from its opening to 8.5, and the only e-mail response he'd received was from a hugely overweight woman in her late thirties who lived fifty miles away—but she was willing to travel.

"Dude, look at her!" Playboy showed Carlos her J-peg. "She looks ready to give birth to a Sumo wrestler."

Pulga countered. "Maybe she *is* a Sumo wrestler."

"Let me see your profile," Carlos said to Playboy.

All the boys leaned over the computer as Playboy clicked to his profile. Below his face pic it read:

USER NAME: *HornyBoy0001.*

DESCRIPTION: *Male, 16 . . .*

Toro remarked, "You're not sixteen yet."

"I will be in a year." Playboy grinned as Carlos kept reading in a low voice: ". . . six feet tall . . ."

Playboy wasn't actually that tall, either. He was about an inch shorter than Carlos.

". . . sexy, VGL . . ." Carlos asked, "What's VGL mean?"

Toro replied, "Volunteers to get laid?"

"That too." Playboy grinned. "It means 'Very Good-Looking.'"

"Better take your photo down," Pulga remarked. "Or they'll see you're lying."

Playboy punched his arm. Carlos continued reading: ". . . hot bod . . . great personality . . . into music (hip hop, house, Los Lonely Boys) . . ."

"You should put that you're a good dancer," Carlos told him.

"You think so?" Playboy said, then decided, "Nah, that's too gay."

Beneath the description, Carlos read the heading LIKES: "Chicks who've got a sexy bod . . . I mean seriously hot! . . . who can get wild and are willing to go out of their way for me."

"Sumo mama is willing to go out of her way," Pulga commented.

"Shut up," Playboy ordered. "She obviously didn't read my 'dis-likes.'"

Under the heading DISLIKES, Carlos read: "Fatties and/or freakishly tall chicks (no offense, Pulga) . . ."

"You jerk!" Pulga socked Playboy's shoulder.

Carlos continued reading: " . . . uglies (don't pretend you're not) . . . stinky chicks . . . stuck-up bitches . . . Internet sluts . . . prudes . . . girls who won't shut up . . . and needy twits."

Carlos finished reading the profile and said, "Hmm."

"What do you mean, 'hmm'?" Playboy asked. "What's wrong with it? Why aren't the hot babes answering?"

"Maybe you should change your picture," Toro suggested.

Playboy frowned, leaning closer to examine his photo. "I look needy, don't I?"

"You look like you need to take a dump," Pulga told him.

"Yeah, *on you!*" Playboy swung out to punch him again, but Pulga ducked.

"Maybe you should use a pic showing your abs," Toro suggested. "That's what a lot of guys do."

He quickly clicked through other boy profiles. About half the guys either had their shirts off or at least pulled up to show their abs.

"You think I should?" Playboy asked Carlos.

"Sure, why not?" Carlos shrugged. "We can use my camera." The digital had been a Christmas present from his ma.

"Here, stand like in this guy's pic." Toro posed Playboy with his shirt lifted up, and his jeans and boxers pulled down to the edge of his pubes.

"You sure this doesn't look gay?" Playboy protested. "I don't want fags e-mailing me."

Carlos peered through the camera screen and recalled Sal scolding him. He now told Playboy, "You shouldn't use the word 'fag.'"

"Oh, that's right," Playboy said sarcastically. "I forgot you're now bi."

"You're bi?" Toro asked. "For real?"

"Shut up," Carlos told Playboy. "I'm not bi."

"Whatever." Playboy rolled his eyes," Just take the picture, *pendejo*."

Carlos took a couple of shots and everyone crowded around to look at them.

"You don't think I look too skinny?" Playboy asked.

"Maybe that'll discourage any more hippos," Pulga suggested.

That idea seemed to satisfy Playboy. After uploading his new photo onto the site, the boys searched through the girl profiles and Playboy e-mailed three chicks he thought were hot.

Carlos felt great spending time with his buds, in spite of the jabs about his turning gay. They'd always teased each other like that anyway. Except now there was a difference: He actually had a gay friend.

Fifteen

CARLOS WAITED TILL Friday, his ma's payday, to tell her, "I need some money for clothes."

She'd just come home from food shopping and he'd quickly offered to put the groceries away.

"I just bought you those sneakers," she replied. "What more clothes do you need?"

Carlos resented having to justify what he wanted money for. It made him feel like one of those needy kids on a "Save the Children" ad. But he recalled how his ma liked Sal, so he told her, "Sal's helping me with my image."

"Your . . . *image*?" His ma smiled at Carlos, her eyes sparkling with interest. "This boy is having quite an influence on you. First your room, now your clothes . . ."

"Yeah," Carlos agreed. Although he'd originally planned to ask his ma for a hundred dollars, her obvious approval of Sal now emboldened him. "I probably need about two hundred bucks."

His ma's eyes suddenly lost their sparkle. "Oh, really? Well, let me just turn the faucet on and see how much money comes out."

That was one of her most annoying expressions.

"I can give you fifty," she countered.

"*Fifty*?" Carlos stopped putting away groceries. "You can hardly buy a pair of underwear for fifty." Besides, Carlos still had to pay Sal his hourly rate and the eighteen dollars he owed him.

"Sorry." His ma resumed putting away groceries.

Carlos reverted to his original target. "Okay, how about a hundred?"

But his ma wouldn't budge. "Fifty."

"Ma, stop being so stingy," Carlos insisted. "How about eighty?"

"I'm not being stingy. I told you what we can afford: fifty."

"Seventy?" Carlos pleaded, helping store a box of macaroni on the top shelf.

"No." His ma's tone grew irritated. "I told you fifty."

Carlos wrapped his arms around her. "Sixty, Ma. Come on, *please*?"

He felt her body relax beneath his embrace. "Okay. Sixty."

Carlos let his arms drop and finished putting away the groceries. Although he'd gotten less money than he'd wanted, at least it was more than his drive-by pa had given him.

Sixteen

SATURDAY MORNING, SAL arrived at eight, but this time Carlos had remembered to set his alarm. In the kitchen over coffee, Sal flirted with Carlos's ma, telling her, "That blouse looks really good on you. It totally highlights your eyes."

"*Gracias*." Mrs. Amoroso beamed. "It's one of my own creations."

"No way!" Sal exclaimed. "You made that? You're really good."

Carlos felt a little weird watching Sal interact with his ma. It didn't give him the creeps like the time Playboy stared at his ma's butt as she bent over the dishwasher. And his ma's liking Sal didn't feel like she was betraying Carlos's pa, like when she got cozy with Raúl. But it did make Carlos feel a little insecure. Was his ma starting to like Sal better than him? Even though Carlos felt silly thinking that, it made him eager to get going that morning.

"Come on," he told Sal as he finished wolfing down his cereal. "Let's go!"

"Your mom's really nice," Sal commented, following Carlos downstairs from the apartment. "So why did your parents split up?"

Carlos gave an evasive shrug. The only people whom he'd told about the reason for the divorce were his buds.

But Sal persisted. "You don't know why your parents broke up?"

Carlos ignored the question, continuing to resist Sal's intrusion. Why did Sal always have to try prying him open? *As soon as this makeover is over,* Carlos thought, *it's really over.*

"Hey, lookit!" Sal stopped walking. "If you want girls to like you,

you're going to have to learn to open up and trust people."

Carlos folded his arms, balking. He saw that Sal's face had the same stern look as when Carlos hadn't wanted to reveal his crush on Roxy. If Carlos didn't open up now, Sal would probably threaten to bail again.

Carlos glanced down at the sidewalk and said in a low voice, "My pa . . . got involved with someone else . . . his secretary . . . and they had a kid." He lifted his eyes to gaze defiantly at Sal. "Now you know. Satisfied?"

"Oh," Sal said gently, laying his hand on Carlos's shoulder. "I'm sorry."

Carlos was keenly aware that it was the first time Sal had touched him. He wasn't sure how he felt about a gay guy touching him. To complicate matters, abruptly and without warning, he felt himself uncontrollably choking up, about to lose it. But why? He'd never cried about his parents' divorce before. His ma had done the crying; he'd struggled to be strong for her.

Now, he swallowed the knot in his throat. "Don't tell anyone what I told you, okay?"

"I won't." Sal gazed at Carlos with that annoying tender look again. "Are you all right?"

"I'm fine." Carlos squirmed out from under Sal's hand. "Can we just go?" He started walking again, before Sal could get a chance to notice the tears brimming in his eyes.

Seventeen

CARLOS HURRIED TOWARD the bus stop ahead of Sal, fighting back his unexpected tears from telling about his pa and Lupita. He struggled to get a grip by focusing on the project at hand—going clothes shopping. "What mall do you want to go to?"

"No mall," Sal called from behind. "We're going downtown to the thrift stores."

"Huh?" Carlos stopped short. "Aren't those stores for poor people? I'm not wearing somebody's smelly rejects."

"Oh, right." Sal caught up alongside him. "I forgot." He gazed down at Carlos's tennis shoes. "You *never* wear anything smelly."

Carlos bristled at the sarcasm, his stifled tears turning to annoyance. "Look, forget it. I don't feel like going shopping anymore. I don't have enough money anyway." He dug into his pocket. "Here." He shoved the crumpled bills toward Sal. "That's what I owe you, plus money for today. I'm going home."

Sal stared at the cash but refused to take it. "What's up with you? Forget the money. You don't have to pay me for today, okay?"

Carlos held the wad of bills in front of him. Why was Sal suddenly letting him off for free? Was it because of what Carlos had told him about the divorce? Carlos didn't want anyone to feel sorry for him. "You said the deal was I had to pay for your time and expenses."

"I know." Sal shook his head. "But you're a friend now. Aren't you?"

Carlos shifted his gaze from Sal to the money and back to Sal. "I've only got seventy bucks. That's all I could get."

"That's plenty!" Sal gestured to his own jeans. "You know how much I paid for these? Ten bucks!"

Carlos eyed the jeans. Earlier, he'd noticed their patchwork of different shades of denim, like something from a designer store—where he could never afford to shop. "Only ten bucks? You sure?"

Sal nodded proudly. "You can borrow them sometime. What size do you wear?"

As they talked, it turned out Carlos and Sal were the same size in everything—waist, inseam, shirts, shoes. Carlos thought: *Freaky*.

"Okay, let's go," he told Sal as the bus pulled up and they climbed on board. "But are you sure they wash the clothes before selling them?"

Eighteen

THEY GOT OFF the bus downtown, in an area Sal called "up-and-coming," though to Carlos it looked down-and-dumpy. Pawnshops, boarded-up storefronts, and iron-grated liquor stores lined the cracked and stained sidewalk. But in between the winos and panhandlers, college students worked on laptops at coffee shops and parents wheeling strollers passed by.

Sal led Carlos into the Sweet Hereafter Thrift Shop. "Let's start with a belt."

"I already have a belt." Carlos lifted his sweatshirt to show Sal.

"I noticed—too blah. Your crotch should communicate intrigue, not boredom."

Intrigue? Carlos wondered. *What the hell does that mean?*

From the rack, Sal pulled a belt with a shiny chrome buckle, emblazoned with one word: SEXY.

Carlos felt the color creep into his cheeks. He could never wear that. Surely everyone would laugh at him. "I'm not wearing that."

"Come on," Sal insisted. "You *are* sexy."

Carlos shifted his feet, wishing Sal wouldn't say stuff like that. "It's the wrong size," he argued.

"Doesn't matter," Sal said, dismantling the SEXY belt. "We're buying it for the buckle. Give me your belt."

Reluctantly, Carlos handed it over. After Sal attached the SEXY buckle, Carlos slid the belt back on and gazed in the mirror. The brazen buckle definitely drew attention toward his crotch—a little too much. Carlos tugged his hoodie hem down over it.

Next they searched for jeans. "They're too picked over," Sal complained. "Let's just switch. Try mine on."

"Are you serious?" Carlos cocked his head.

Sal pressed him toward the side-by-side dressing rooms and passed the jeans over the partition. Carlos shuffled out and peered cautiously into the mirror. Between the SEXY buckle and stylish jeans, he *did* look kind of sexy—at least from the waist down.

"You're definitely keeping those." Sal pointed to the jeans. "They give you an awesome bubble butt and a great package."

Carlos's cheeks flared hot. Did Sal have to keep saying crap like that?

"Now, what's with this green hoodie you always wear?" Sal asked. "Are you trying to blend into the school lockers? It's no wonder girls don't notice you."

Carlos had never thought of it that way. All he knew was the sweatshirt made him feel . . . safe.

"I like wearing it."

"It makes you look like a lurker." Sal frowned. "Take it off for a sec."

"I'm not taking it off." Carlos shoved his fists into the hoodie's pockets. But Sal glared back at him, unyielding. "Oh, screw it!" Carlos yanked down his hood, tore open the zipper, and peeled out of the sleeves. "Satisfied?"

He rammed his hands into his jean pockets while Sal commented, "I don't know why you hide beneath that sweat rag. You've got a nice frame—and great nips."

Carlos finally exploded. "Would you stop saying that crap?" He reached for his sweatshirt again, but Sal snatched it out of reach.

"Easy, boy. I told you, I already have a boyfriend, so relax. Now, come on, let's find you a shirt."

Grudgingly, Carlos followed, crossing his arms. Without his hoodie he felt naked, exposed.

"They're two for fifteen bucks," Sal announced, plunging his hand into a rack of shirts and pulling out a black polo. Carlos actually liked the shirt, but then Sal also yanked out a pink one. "Here, try this on."

"I'm not wearing pink. What's wrong with the black one?"

"First try this. Girls *love* guys in pink. It makes you look sensitive."

"It'll make me look like a—" He started to say something but changed his mind. "Like a wimp."

Sal held the shirt out. "You *are* a wimp, or you'd try it on."

Carlos clenched his jaw. There seemed to be no winning against Sal. He took the pink shirt into the dressing room, giving it a precautionary sniff. When he stepped out to the mirror, he thought the shirt looked totally gay.

"It makes you look sure of yourself," Sal nodded approvingly. "Leave it on."

"Whatever." Carlos rolled his eyes, going along, but, heading out of the thrift shop, he pulled his hoodie back on.

"Hey, what're you doing?" Sal protested.

"I feel naked without it!"

"Okay." Sal studied him as they walked. "I've got an idea. Let's try this store."

Inside the shop, Sal headed straight for the denim section. From a rack, he pulled out a jean jacket. "Here!" He held it up for Carlos and spoke like a British butler. "Classic Levi's, sir. Please kindly try it on."

Carlos sighed, unzipped his hoodie, and slid his arms into the soft denim jacket.

"Whoa, studly!" Sal gave a long whistle. "It gives you megashoulders."

"Shut up," Carlos said under his breath. But as he peered in the mirror, he couldn't deny that the jacket made his shoulders look bigger. Plus, it helped hide the pink shirt. Altogether, he did look kind of . . . studly.

"You really think I should get it?"

Sal gave a sly grin. "You're not walking out of here without it."

At the register, Carlos found that even after buying the jacket, he still had cash left. "Hey," he told Sal. "Why don't we get *you* something?"

Sal stared at him, his face taking on that annoying tender look again. "Thanks, but no. This is your day. Besides, we still need to get you a wallet, remember?"

They found a really nice black leather one, with chrome studs at the corners, for only five bucks. Carlos couldn't get over how cheap everything was—and how none of it smelled. He felt happy about his new used clothes, with little thanks to his stingy pa.

"Crap!" He checked Sal's watch: almost noon. "I forgot about my pa!"

He'd never forgotten his pa before. Granted, he was usually home on Saturday mornings, so he couldn't forget. Would his pa now go up to the apartment for him—and actually talk to Carlos's ma face-to-face?

Quickly, Carlos yanked Sal out of the store. It was only after they'd boarded the bus that Carlos realized he'd inadvertently left his hoodie behind. But it was too late to go back.

Nineteen

As CARLOS RACED across his apartment parking lot, he spotted his pa leaning on his car's hood, while Lupita and Henry waited inside the car.

"Glad you finally decided to show up." His pa glanced up from his watch at Carlos's pink shirt and jean jacket. "What're you wearing? You look like a *maricón*."

Carlos cringed—not so much because his pa had called him a *maricón*, but because beside him stood Sal.

"Hurry up and get your stuff," his pa ordered. "If you're not back in five minutes, I leave without you."

Carlos hurried up the building staircase, even though he half-wished his pa *would* leave without him.

"Hmm," Sal murmured. "I wonder which side of the family you get your homophobia from."

Inside the apartment, Carlos's ma was fitting a sewing client in the living room. "Carlos, your pa phoned so angry. What happened?"

"I forgot!" Carlos grumbled, rushing past.

"Wait!" his ma called. "Let me look at you." Her gaze glided from shoulders to toes. "Very nice!" She beamed at Sal. "You're a good influence on him."

"Thanks." Sal grinned.

Inside his bedroom, Carlos grabbed clean underwear, a schoolbook, and his toothbrush, stuffing them into his backpack. Outside, his pa's horn blared.

"Shut up," Carlos muttered, and turned to Sal. "Hey, thanks for your help today."

"*No problema.* Sorry I wasn't watching the time."

"I don't care," Carlos replied, leading Sal from the bedroom. "He's always late. Now, suddenly he's Mister Punctuality."

As they bounded down the staircase, Sal asked, "Same time next Saturday? We'll work on your grooming."

"Huh?" Carlos stopped at the bottom landing. "What's 'grooming' mean?"

Sal rolled his eyes. "You are *so* not gay."

After saying "laters," Carlos climbed into the car's backseat next to Henry.

"Next time I'm not waiting," his pa groused, starting the engine.

"Don't wait," Carlos muttered. "I don't give a shit."

His pa shot Carlos a sharp look in the rearview mirror but didn't say anything. Apparently, he hadn't heard Carlos, or he was pretending he hadn't. Carlos kind of hoped he *had* heard him. He was sick of the same stupid routine each weekend. Why did he put himself through it? Only to remind himself how much his life had changed—for the worse? He was starting to accept that it was never going back to like it used to be.

That evening, they all sat around the TV in his pa's apartment, watching some dumb G-rated movie, with Henry sitting on his pa's lap. Carlos didn't want to waste his weekends this way anymore. But how could he tell his pa that?

Twenty

MONDAY MORNING, CARLOS pulled his new clothes on and examined his reflection in the dresser mirror. The SEXY buckle definitely drew attention to what Sal had called his "package." He turned sideways and glanced over his shoulder at his butt. Before, he'd believed it was too flat. But not in these jeans. Beneath the black polo shirt, he noticed the bumps of his nipples. He'd always thought they poked out too much, but, given Sal's reaction, he wondered: Might girls actually be attracted by them? More to the point, would Roxy be?

He felt like the proverbial butterfly, about to burst from its cocoon. He wondered, though, what his caterpillar friends would say.

He stepped onto the school bus and braced himself. Toro was first to notice. "Where's your hoodie?"

"Sexy?" Playboy smirked at Carlos's buckle. "Where's the 'not' part?"

Pulga reached up and tweaked Carlos's nipple. "Got milk?"

The guys brayed like jackasses while Carlos gazed out the window, waiting for them to get over it. At last, Playboy moaned, "I'm down to a six on Hot-or-Snot. Can someone please tell me how that's possible?"

"Because you're a *pendejo*?" Pulga offered.

Playboy kicked Pulga's bus seat. "I bet some chick I rejected is trying to snot me. I mean, I've got good abs, don't I?"

"Yeah, you do," Toro reassured him.

But Playboy slouched down in his seat, folding his arms. "That site is for losers who get off on giving people 'ones.'"

"Then why are you on it?" Carlos asked.

Playboy stared at him like he was crazy. "You realize how many millions of babes visit that site? I've got to get lucky *sometime*."

Carlos pondered that for a sec, but as their bus neared school, his thoughts returned to his new clothes and Roxy. Would she notice him now?

He looked for her after second period but she was nowhere in sight. At lunch, when he finally spotted her, she was busy with her friends. So, he decided that, after last bell, he'd casually stroll past her locker.

When the time came, she was talking with her group again, diminishing the chance that she'd notice him. Nevertheless, he took a deep breath and walked in her direction. His legs felt like Jell-O beneath him. Without his hoodie, he felt so naked that he almost hoped she *wouldn't* notice him. But just as he walked past, somehow, miraculously, she glanced toward him.

From across the hall, her dazzling green eyes scanned down his clothes. And beneath Carlos's new shirt and jacket, his heart leaped in his chest.

He opened his mouth, wanting desperately to speak. But he'd been so certain she wouldn't even see him that he hadn't prepared anything to say. The most he could manage was to raise his hand and give a dorky little wave.

And yet, to his amazement, as Roxy's gaze reached his SEXY belt buckle, a foxy little smile crinkled at the corners of her mouth. Her gaze ascended to his eyes. Then she raised her hand and waved back.

Granted, it was only for an instant before she returned to her friends. But that didn't matter. She had noticed him.

Carlos nearly danced down the hall as he headed toward his bus.

Twenty-One

As soon as Carlos got home, he phoned Sal. "You won't believe it: Dude, she waved to me!"

"Awesome!" Sal cheered as Carlos told him all about it.

When Carlos finally calmed down enough to stop talking, Sal announced, "Hey, I've got news for you, too. I got us an appointment with Harris to discuss the GSA."

Still lingering in his Roxy haze, it took Carlos a moment to recall who Harris was: Lone Star High's principal.

"We're meeting with him," Sal continued, "after school tomorrow. Okay?"

In truth, Carlos had been so focused on the makeover part of their deal that he'd put any thought of the GSA out of his mind.

"Um, so you want me to go too?" he now asked.

"Duh!" Sal's voice sounded irritated. "Of course! I need you to talk—as the straight guy in the group—about how homophobia hurts everybody."

Carlos pondered that. "But I don't know what to say."

"Sure you do! You get called 'faggot' too, don't you?"

"Yeah. Everyone does sometimes."

"Exactly! And do you like being called 'homo' or '*maricón*'?"

"No."

"Then why don't you do something about it?"

"Because it's like being called '*pendejo*'—it doesn't really mean anything."

"Oh, yeah? If it's the same as being called 'pendejo,' then why are you scared to be seen with me? Why are you so afraid people might think you're gay?"

Carlos bit into his lip, unsure how to respond.

Sal continued. "Homophobia means that, any time you say or do anything the least bit different, you risk getting called queer—whether you are or not. You think that doesn't hurt you? You think that doesn't keep you from being an individual?"

Carlos's brain was starting to ache. "I guess so."

"All right, then," Sal said triumphantly. "That's what I want you to talk about tomorrow. I'm counting on you, okay?"

Carlos ran a hand through his hair and mumbled, "Yeah, okay."

"Don't sound so enthusiastic," Sal said sarcastically.

In fact, Carlos wasn't enthusiastic. After hanging up, he laid down in bed, his head throbbing from the conversation. In addition, he now had a new worry: Would Principal Harris think he was gay?

Twenty-Two

THE FOLLOWING DAY, Carlos didn't tell his friends about his after-school GSA commitment. When the final bell rang, he bolted to the main office and slinked inside, wishing he still had his sweatshirt. In its place, he pulled the collar of his jean jacket up and watched the steady stream of staff and students hustle in and out the main door.

A girl wearing an orange hoodie wandered in, scanning the room as if expecting someone. Beneath her hood, she looked vaguely familiar and cute—not Roxy gorgeous, but definitely cute—with a sprinkle of freckles and soft hazel eyes. Carlos averted his gaze while trying to recollect where he'd seen her. When he glanced shyly up at her, a little smile squiggled onto her face, bright as sunshine. Carlos felt his cheeks flame. Instantly, he recalled her from the library, with Sal and—

Carlotta, Pulga's ceiling-tall benefit-friend, strode into the reception room. Carlos sank farther into his seat. Was she also helping to start the GSA? Carlos hadn't counted on that. No doubt she'd blab to Pulga she'd seen Carlos, and he'd get even more crap from his buds.

"Hi, Espie!" Carlotta waved at Hoodie Girl. "Are we the first ones here? Oh, hi, Carlos!"

Just then, Freaky Vicky traipsed through the door, dressed weird as ever: camouflage pants, military dog tags, combat boots, and a T-shirt that read: MAKE WAR NOT LOVE.

"Hey, gang!" Sal followed behind her. "Has anyone seen . . ." He spotted Carlos. "Oh, there you are. I'll let them know we're all here."

He spoke to the secretary behind the counter and signaled the group. "Come on, troops!"

Inside his office, the principal sat behind his huge metal desk like it was some sort of battle tank, armored with papers. "Hard-Ass Harris," as students called him, was an ex-Army captain with a flattop haircut and a voice that boomed cannonlike through the halls, ordering students to class.

"Take a seat," he now commanded Carlos's group, but there were only four chairs facing his desk.

Carlos seized the opportunity to hang back, hoping to blend into the wall.

But Sal glanced over his shoulder at him. "Come sit up here. I'll stand."

"I'm fine back here," Carlos assured him, and plopped onto the vinyl couch.

Sal shot him a peeved look as Mr. Harris braced his hands on top of his desk. "So what's this all about?"

Sal turned to face him. "We want to start a Gay-Straight Alliance."

Mr. Harris's brow furrowed into trenches. "You mean a club for *homosexuals*?" He pronounced the word as if speaking a foreign language.

"No . . ." Sal's voice resonated with irritation. "I mean a club where *all* students can talk about homophobia and get support."

Carlotta spoke out in agreement. "I'm not gay, but I have friends who are. And I know what it's like to be made fun of."

Vicky followed. "It's hard to feel safe in school when people constantly call you names like 'lesbo' and 'dyke.'"

"Some students," Espie added more softly, "have gay relatives and no place that feels safe to talk about it."

"That's all well and good." Mr. Harris moved a stack of papers from the right flank of his desk to the left. "But I can't allow a club that condones immorality."

"Immorality?" Sal rose up in his seat. "What's immoral is letting people get harassed and not doing anything to stop it." He jabbed his finger like a bayonet toward Mr. Harris. *"That's* immoral!"

Carlos watched from the rear, sitting up with interest. He'd come into the meeting secretly kind of hoping the group's application would be denied so that he could avoid getting involved altogether, but now he almost hoped they'd win.

Mr. Harris glowered at Sal. "You're out of line, son."

"Mr. Harris?" Carlotta interceded. "I think what Sal is trying to say is, this group will help protect people."

"All day long," Vicky added, "you walk down the hall and hear people say, 'That's so gay,' 'She's so queer.'"

Espie agreed. "You wouldn't let people say racial or religious stuff that way, like 'That's so black' or 'She's so Baptist.'"

"I appreciate your concerns," Mr. Harris said to the girls—and it seemed to Carlos that he shifted the same stack of papers he'd previously moved from the left back to the right. "But I believe a group like this would only be disruptive. I can't allow that."

"Other schools have GSAs," Sal countered. "They're not disruptive."

"What other schools do is their business," Mr. Harris fired back. "I'm responsible for my school. And I say no."

"But you've got to!" Sal shouted.

Mr. Harris stood to face him. "Son, I said no. You're dismissed!"

The room fell silent as the girls and Sal stood to leave. But Carlos squirmed in his seat, waiting for someone to correct Mr. Harris. According to the GSA websites he'd originally researched, a school did indeed *have* to allow a GSA, whether the principal liked it or not. Surely Sal knew that—didn't he? Then why wasn't he speaking up?

Carlos clenched his jaw, trying to keep quiet. After all, this club was Sal's problem, not his. But the words burst uncontrollably from

Carlos's mouth. "Mr. Harris? Actually, um, you *do* have to let us have the club."

The group stopped their retreat. All eyes turned toward Carlos. The seconds stretched interminably as Mr. Harris's brow furrowed even deeper.

"Didn't you hear what I said?" Mr. Harris's words rattled like a machine gun.

"Yes, sir." Carlos jammed his hands into his pockets, trying to keep from trembling. "But, um, according to the ACLU.org site—that's the American Civil Liberties Union—because of, um, a Supreme Court decision about something called the Federal Equal Access Act, you *have* to allow the club." Carlos swallowed the lump in his throat. "Even if you think it's immoral."

Sal stared at Carlos, his frustrated scowl slowly turning upward into a smile. Then he triumphantly pivoted to face Mr. Harris—who looked like he'd just been shot.

Twenty-Three

THE LITTLE TROOP marched victoriously from the principal's office, praising Carlos as a hero.

"You were awesome!" Espie grinned.

"Yeah, wait till I tell Pulga!" Carlotta remarked.

"You were like our secret weapon!" Sal clapped Carlos on the back. "Why didn't you tell me that ACLU stuff before?"

Carlos shrugged. "I thought you knew."

Even Vicky stopped glowering, apparently starting to forgive him.

And yet Carlos felt like he'd sort of shot himself in the foot, having blown his best chance to dodge the GSA. Why hadn't he just kept his mouth shut?

Granted, Mr. Harris hadn't fully said yes to the GSA, but he'd clearly been taken aback, shuffling papers on his desk and saying, "I'll take the matter up with the superintendent."

Meanwhile, Carlos wondered, how would he explain this to his friends?

Friday evening, he and his buds hung out at Pulga's house, sprawling on the carpet, eating pizza, and playing video games. Carlos waited anxiously, hoping the GSA would escape mention. But Pulga brought it up: "Hey, Carlotta said you whipped Harris's ass at some meeting for that gay group."

"It's not a gay group," Carlos corrected, "or Carlotta wouldn't be in it, would she?"

"Is Carlotta bi?" Playboy asked Pulga excitedly. "Dude, you should get her to do a three-way—two babes at once!"

"I wish!" Pulga told Playboy. "But she's not bi. I already asked."

"You stood up to Hard-Ass Harris?" Toro asked Carlos, glancing up from the muscle mag he'd been reading.

"Sort of. I guess so. I just told him the law says he has to allow the group."

"Yeah, great, genius," Pulga moaned. "Thanks to you, now Carlotta is trying to get me to join the group. Every day she gets more bossy, like she thinks she's my girlfriend. Tomorrow she wants me to go to a movie with her."

"You mean, like a date?" Playboy shook his head with disapproval. "You'd better nip that in the bud right away."

"How?" Pulga moaned. "I don't want to give up the sex."

The boys became silent, listening to a Los Lonely Boys CD, and Carlos's thoughts turned to Roxy. Would she one day go to a movie with him? He didn't completely get why Pulga and Playboy were so against having a real girlfriend, but he didn't want to ask and seem stupid, either.

Playboy stood from the carpet. "I want to check my Hot-or-Snot rating."

"What for?" Carlos tried to dissuade him. "It'll only make you feel bad."

"You don't know that." Playboy strode over to Pulga's computer. "It might've gone up."

But his rating had actually declined even further—sinking below the "five" threshold.

"No!" Playboy slammed the mouse down. "This can't be happening. I'm not snot!"

"Hey, chill, man!" Pulga gave his shoulder a soothing pat, but Playboy shoved him away.

As the boys crowded around, he switched to the girls' profiles, rating each with a "one."

"*They're* doing this to me. They're all bitches!"

"Take it easy, dude." Toro intervened, trying to pry the mouse from Playboy's hand.

But Playboy brushed him off too, continuing to click photos. "Take that, bitch! See how it feels, bitch!"

"Dude, calm down," Carlos urged, when suddenly, unexpectedly, the computer screen flashed a familiar green-eyed girl.

"STOP!" Carlos shouted so loud the boys froze—even Playboy. Carlos yanked the mouse from his hand and leaned over the monitor, unable to believe his eyes. Staring back from the screen at him was USERNAME: *GlitterGirl*. But the photo was unmistakably Roxy.

DESCRIPTION: *5'6"ish, blonde highlights, green/brown/or blue eyes (depending on my mood) . . . single . . . available (hint-hint) . . . a cheerleader . . . fun kind of girl . . . and I'm not lez so guys plz stop asking, ok?*

Carlos's heart raced ahead of him as his gaze sped across the screen.

LIKES: *First off, I like boys! . . .*

Good. So far, Carlos qualified.

. . . who are kinda smart (but not nerdy) . . .

"You guys think I'm nerdy?" Carlos asked his friends as they leaned over his shoulder.

"Nah," Pulga replied. "Definitely a *pendejo*, but not nerdy."

. . . guys who are nice, sweet, have a good sense of humor, cute smile . . .

"I'm all that, aren't I?" Carlos asked.

"I think you are," Toro replied.

"You two *are* going gay, aren't you?" Playboy quipped, but Carlos kept reading.

. . . a boy who likes me for ME and is actually interested in ME! not just in wanting to get into my pants . . .

Carlos wondered: Who on Earth could possibly be more interested in her than him? Although he'd like to get into her pants too.

DISLIKES: *Selfish, uncaring, unhonest guys . . . Fakes and phonies, especially girls (ugh, that annoys me) . . . Ppl that give me 1's (I'm not that ugly, am I?)*

Carlos couldn't imagine anybody giving Roxy a one, except some bitter maniac like the friend next to him.

. . . guys who just want sex . . . pervs, creeps, and annoying needy guys (get a life!)

Carlos breathed a sigh of relief. Nothing he'd read had ruled him out. Yet even so, little blisters of nervous sweat began beading on his forehead.

"You going to e-mail her?" Pulga asked.

"Um, not right now." Carlos quickly rated her a ten before Playboy could give her any less.

But Playboy had calmed down, moving to the mirror to study a blemish. "How can she have a nine-point-eight and I'm a four-point-eight?"

"She's got better boobs," Pulga answered.

Playboy threw a hairbrush from the dresser at him, but Pulga ducked.

"It's getting late." Carlos faked a yawn. "I'm heading home."

"Nah, don't go," Toro urged. "Let's watch a DVD."

"You *pendejos* want to spend the night?" Pulga asked.

"I can't," Carlos replied. "I've got to get up early tomorrow."

"For what?" Playboy flashed Carlos a glance in the mirror. "You got a brunch date with your boyfriend?"

Carlos froze. Had his friends somehow found out about his Saturday mornings with Sal? Quickly, he replied, "My pa's picking me up early."

Playboy pulled himself from the mirror and wrapped an arm around Carlos's shoulder. "Hey," he whispered in his ear. "Promise, when you get home, you'll give me a ten. Okay, buddy?"

"Sure." Carlos patted him on the back, feeling kind of sorry for him. Although at times he wondered if Playboy had any feelings at all—unless you considered horniness a feeling—in other moments (like now), it seemed there was more to Playboy than his swaggering exterior suggested.

When Carlos arrived home, he did as he'd promised. Then he searched for Roxy's profile. After giving her another ten, he stared at her picture on the screen for a good half hour, fighting an urge to kiss it. That would be way too silly.

And yet, as he undressed, the urge grew uncontrollable. He clicked off the light, crept across the darkness to the monitor and tapped his lips to the screen, feeling supremely harebrained. Then he climbed into bed and, after a series of contented moans, drifted into dreamland.

Twenty-Four

SATURDAY MORNING, CARLOS answered the door expecting Sal, but found that Sal had also brought along another boy who appeared to be the same age, though shorter and more muscled.

"This is Javier, my boyfriend."

Carlos's brain reverberated with the word "boyfriend." Although he recalled Sal mentioning it, the reality of an actual live person had never sunk in—till now.

Having a gay *couple* in his home seemed almost too much to handle. He was now outnumbered. And besides, Sal was supposed to keep their makeover sessions a secret. On top of all that, Carlos felt something totally unexpected: He didn't want to share Sal. He'd grown to enjoy his time with Sal *alone*.

"'S'up?" Carlos shook hands with Javier, while giving Sal a sideways glare.

But Sal didn't seem to notice. "Javi is in cosmetology school—a hair master. I told him how you stood up to Harris and he wanted to meet you—your reward for helping out."

Lucky me, Carlos thought. He led the boys to his bedroom, feeling even more uncomfortable when Javier whispered, "You're right, he's cute," and Sal replied, "Didn't I tell you?"

"Hey, nice job with the room," Javier exclaimed. He dropped his backpack onto Carlos's bed and strode over to the praying mantis. "So this is the bug?"

Carlos gritted his teeth. How much had Sal told Javier?

"That's her!" Sal replied, rolling Carlos's desk chair in front of the dresser mirror. "So, should we start with hair or face first?" he asked Javier, while guiding Carlos into the chair.

It was all making Carlos feel weirdly out of place in his own room.

"Let's begin with a face mask." Javier pulled a series of tubes and bottles from his backpack. "First, we need to cleanse his pores."

"You're all bottled up inside," Sal agreed, draping a towel around Carlos's neck, while Javier smeared a cold, grainy paste onto Carlos's cheeks, caking his face till only his eyes peered out, raccoonlike.

Carlos tried to sit still, while growing uncomfortably warm. He wasn't accustomed to having somebody else touch his face—especially some gay dude he'd barely met. "Um, will this get rid of my zits?"

"It'll definitely help," Javier told him. "You need to do this once a week. I'll leave the can with you."

Meanwhile, Sal took hold of Carlos's hand. "We've really got to work on your nails. They're one of the first things a girl looks at."

Javier nodded in agreement. "Who knows why they're so obsessed with guys' hands, but they are."

"First you clip down to the pink," Sal explained, snipping away with a pair of nail clippers. "Fingernails should be rounded. Toenails can be straighter. Give me your other hand."

Carlos switched hands and Javier pulled out an emery board, filing the trimmed nails. "After you clip, then you smooth them down."

Carlos stared in the mirror at the two gay guys holding his hands. Maybe it was better to close his eyes.

"Does he know about cuticles?" Javier asked. Carlos cracked one eye open again.

"Oh, good point," Sal replied, and explained to Carlos about taking care of cuticles and hangnails. Then Javier grabbed several bottles from his backpack and led Carlos to the bathroom to wash off the face mask.

As the three boys crowded in around the sink, Javier explained: "Now, here's what you do on a daily basis: First, you use a gentle foaming cleanser to wash away dirt without taking away your necessary oils. That's this one." He held up a white bottle. "Use it twice a day, when you wake up and before you go to bed. Do it now to practice."

While Carlos massaged the foam into his face, Javier pulled out a clear bottle. "Good. Now, after that, use a mild toner. Witch hazel is cheap, natural, and fragrance-free. It'll help contract those large, unsightly pores and get rid of residues your cleanser couldn't."

Carlos wiped his face outside, while inside, his head was swimming. Did the straight guys on *Queer Eye* feel this uncomfortable? How would he ever remember all this?

As if reading his mind, Sal reassured him. "Don't worry, we'll write down instructions."

"Last . . ." Javier brought out a jar. "You use an oil-free moisturizer. I know that sounds girly, but your skin will thank you."

"And remember," Sal broke in, "the best moisturizer is water. You need to drink at least eight to ten glasses a day. Not Coke or coffee—*water*."

"Does he take vitamins?" Javier asked Sal, and Sal looked at Carlos.

"Sometimes," Carlos mumbled.

"You should take a multivitamin every day," Javier told him, "to help replenish your skin. Now, ready to work on your hair?"

They returned to the bedroom. While Carlos and Sal spread an old bedsheet on the carpet, Javier pulled from his backpack scissors, a comb, and electric clippers. Sal sat Carlos down in the chair again and Javier redraped the towel around Carlos's neck, gazing in the mirror at him. "So, now, what's your vision for your hair?"

"Huh?" Carlos stared back at him.

"He means," Sal clarified, "is there anything you've always wanted to do with your hair?"

Carlos thought for a moment, then sat up excitedly. "Can you shave my initials into the back of my head?" He'd always thought that looked tough on guys.

Sal and Javier peered in the mirror at him, eyes aghast. Simultaneously, they replied, "No!"

Javier turned to Sal. "Here's what I'm thinking . . ." He ran his fingers through Carlos's hair. "Short on the sides and choppy on top so he can spike or tousle."

"Exactly," Sal agreed. "And a little longer in front?"

"Yeah, that's it! Let's start with the sides. Do you think a two or a three?"

Sal handed him the clippers. "Start with a three. We can always go down to a two."

Javier clipped the sides, then sprayed the top of Carlos's hair with water and snipped quickly with scissors, twirling the shears between his fingers. He made it appear so easy.

"Is it hard to cut hair?" Carlos asked.

"Yeah, at first . . . I began when I was eight—by trying to give our Pekingese a new hairstyle. When I showed my sister, she said Mom was going to kill me."

Carlos glanced down at his own cut hair, suddenly feeling a little nervous.

"I hid in the laundry room," Javier continued, "crying hysterically while I tried to glue back Ming-Ming's hair. But when Mom found me, she only laughed."

He turned to Sal. "Gel or pomade?"

"I'd go with wax." Sal handed Javier a jar. "He's got wicked thick hair."

"Excellent!" Javier dipped his finger into the jar and told Carlos, "Now, when you work this into your hair, always start with the back, so you don't forget."

Carlos peered in the mirror, relieved and amazed. His new haircut made him look almost like some TV teen idol.

But Javier wasn't satisfied. "It still needs something." He tapped his fingertips on his chin, pondering Carlos's hair. "Hmm. Tell me about this girl you're so hot for."

Carlos sighed. Was there anything Sal *hadn't* told Javier?

"Want to see her picture?" Carlos offered. "Just click on the computer."

Sal clicked the mouse and Roxy's Hot-or-Snot J-peg appeared as the screensaver.

"She's got great hair." Javier turned to Sal. "You know, why don't we—?"

"Oh, my God!" Sal interrupted. "Highlights! Totally!" He turned to Carlos. "Have you got tin foil?"

"Um . . ." Carlos squirmed in his chair, unsure about highlights. He already looked better than before. Maybe he should quit while ahead. Besides, his friends always put down guys who streaked their hair, saying, "That's so gay."

"You'll definitely get Roxy's attention," Sal said coaxingly.

A half hour later Carlos was getting his hair streaked when the phone rang.

"Carlitos!" his ma yelled from the living room. "It's your pa!"

Carlos quickly glanced at the clock. He'd forgotten about his pa—again. He was having fun with Sal and Javier—a lot more fun than he'd have with Lupita and Henry. But could he tell his pa that? He didn't want to hurt his feelings.

A little nervously, he answered the phone. "Um, 'S'up?"

"*Mi'jo*," his pa said. "You going to be ready this time?" He didn't say it in a mean way, but even so, it bothered Carlos.

"Um . . ." Carlos's voice trembled. "I don't think I can come today."

The line became silent. Then his pa asked, "Is something wrong, *mi'jo?*"

"No, I've just got stuff to do." That wasn't totally a lie: Javier and Sal were still streaking his hair.

The line turned quiet again. "Okay," his pa said at last. "See you next weekend."

Carlos stared at the phone, trying to sort out his mixed-up feelings. On one hand, he was glad not to have to endure another boring visit. But at the same time, he couldn't deny the ache inside his chest.

Twenty-Five

AFTER CARLOS HUNG up the phone, Sal asked, "You okay?"

"Huh?" Carlos suddenly realized he'd zoned out. "Um, yeah. I'm okay."

As Javier continued to streak Carlos's hair, Sal asked, "How come you don't want to go with your dad?"

Carlos didn't want to talk about it, especially with Javier present. Nevertheless, he could almost bet Sal would somehow make him open up about it.

"Because it's boring!" he sputtered. "He spends the whole time with his new wife and kid. It used to be just him and me."

"Oh." Sal gently unwrapped the tin foil from Carlos's hair. "Have you told him you'd like him to spend time with just you?"

"No," Carlos grumbled. "Why should I have to tell him that?"

"Well," Javier interjected, "otherwise how will he know?"

Carlos clenched his jaw, feeling like they were ganging up on him. "Look, if he wanted to spend time with me, he would. Besides, he'll probably say my hair looks like a *maricón*."

Sal and Javier winced. Carlos felt sorry for saying it, but at least they shut up about his pa. And yet, he found himself considering what they'd said. Should he say something to his pa?

While he thought about it, Sal and Javier finished doing his hair. Carlos stared in awe at the mirror. The shiny blond streaks made him look like a different person: Confident. Cool . . .

He leaped from the chair. "I want to show my ma!" He ran down the hall to the living room, Sal and Javier right behind him.

His ma was fitting their neighbor, Mrs. Bustamante, in a dress. Both women stared at Carlos and nodded approval. "Bravo!" Mrs. Amoroso commented to Sal and Javier.

"Can you boys do my hair?" Mrs. Bustamante asked. "How much do you charge?"

Javier smiled proudly. "I'm not allowed to charge till I have my license. But I can do it for you at my school."

"Carlitos?" His ma glanced at her watch. "Isn't your pa coming?"

"Um, no. I'm not going with him."

His ma stopped smiling. "*¿Por qué?*"

"'Cause I don't feel like it!" The words came out harsher than he'd intended.

The room was silent as everyone stared at him.

"Well," Sal said at last. "Javi and I are going to lunch." He turned toward Carlos. "You want to come with us?"

Carlos shrugged. Although he'd like to go with them, he had zero money.

"Here . . ." His ma pulled some bills from her purse. "Why don't you treat the boys for doing such a nice job on your hair?"

Carlos gladly took the money, relieved to drop the issue of his pa.

Javier collected his stuff, Sal wrote down instructions for everything they'd told Carlos, and the boys headed outside.

It turned out that Javier had his own car—not a new one, but still . . . It was more than any of Carlos's buds had.

As he hopped into the back of the Camry, Carlos asked, "How many miles does she have?"

"Ninety thousand." Javier started the car and pulled out onto the street. "It's in pretty good shape except for a rattle when I turn to the left. Listen . . ." As he changed lanes, the left side of the car clunked.

"It sounds like an axle." Carlos had learned about cars from talking to the guys at his ma's job and conversations with her boyfriend, Raúl. "I'll take a look when we park."

As they drove, Carlos saw between the front seats that Javier took hold of Sal's hand. Carlos squirmed on the backseat. Two guys holding hands wasn't something he'd seen before—unless you counted field-trip buddies in second grade, when all the boys had to hold hands. But obviously that was different . . . or was it? Why was it okay for two little boys to hold hands but it made him uneasy if it was two teenage guys?

He thought about that and decided to ask about something else on his mind. "Do you think a gay person can change?"

Sal gave an exasperated groan, but Javier squeezed his hand as if to calm him and glanced in the rearview at Carlos. "It's like your hair color. You can streak it blond, but it's still brown underneath."

Carlos looked in the mirror at his highlighted hair, suddenly once again worried how his friends might react.

"Or like being left-handed," Javier continued. "Can some left-handed people learn to use their right hand? Sure, but that doesn't change their being left-handed. And besides, what's the point?"

"That's the real issue," Sal interjected. "Why do some people get so bent out of shape about anyone who's different? Who cares whether somebody else loves someone of the opposite sex or the same sex? They think that gives them the right to bash us and treat us like crap?"

Javier squeezed Sal's hand again. Then he pulled into the parking lot of a restaurant.

Once out of the car, Carlos slid beneath the chassis and checked the axle. "Yep, you can see the grease leaking. My ma's boyfriend works at a garage. I'll ask him to look at it if you want."

"Great!" Javier exclaimed.

The restaurant was a health food café that smelled of yeasty fresh bread. College students, yuppies, ponytailed older guys, and beaded women filled the place. Their waitress looked college-age, with bright blue eyes. "I like your hair," she told Carlos.

He darted his gaze down at the menu, blushing. "Um, I'll have the veggie burger."

Sal and Javier both ordered salads. After the waitress left, Sal told Carlos in a low voice, "Hey, when someone compliments you, say, 'Thanks.'"

Carlos turned even redder. How was he supposed to know that? Hardly anyone had ever complimented him—until recently.

When the waitress brought their order, Carlos told her, "Um, thanks for what you said about my hair."

She gave him a big smile. "You're welcome, honey."

Sweat exploded from his pores. Had she actually called him "honey"?

As she walked away, Sal and Javier grinned at Carlos. "It looks like you have a fan."

"Shut up." Carlos grabbed hold of his burger, eyeing the waitress, then asked, "You think so?"

As he ate, another thing he'd wondered about came to mind: "How did you two guys meet?"

"On the Internet," Javier replied.

"At a matchup dating site," Sal added.

Carlos's mind instantly leaped to Hot-or-Snot. "You mean a hookup?"

"No." Sal frowned. "Not a hookup. A date."

Carlos put down his burger. "What's the difference?"

"We spent time getting to know each other first," Sal explained. "Before we had sex."

Carlos shifted in his seat. He had zero desire to hear anything about two guys having sex. But he was curious about one thing: "Didn't you ever want to have sex with a girl?"

"Ew!" Sal exclaimed. "No way!"

But Javier said, "I actually did once."

"Oh, God!" Sal rolled his eyes. "Do we have to talk about this over lunch?"

"Cover your ears!" Javier retorted and turned to Carlos. "It was sophomore year, with my best friend Sheila . . . She knew I liked guys, but we both decided I should try it with a girl first. So we did."

Sal stuck his finger down his throat as if to make himself puke.

"And what happened?" Carlos asked.

"It felt, like, unnatural," Javier replied. "Outside, the plumbing worked, but inside it felt all wrong. It's just not who I am."

"Hel-lo!" Sal exclaimed. "I could've told you that."

Javier grinned at Sal. In spite of their teasing, it was plain how much they liked each other.

That's what I want with a girl, Carlos thought.

When the check came, he said, "My treat," and pulled out the money his ma had given him.

"Thanks," the boys said. As they pulled out of the parking lot, Sal glanced in the backseat at Carlos. "Hey, you want to come work out with us at the rec center?"

"Um, sure." He didn't have anything else planned, and working out seemed like the next logical step in his makeover. Besides, he was enjoying Sal and Javier. It even stopped troubling him when they held hands.

Twenty-Six

THE BOYS STOPPED to get Carlos's gym clothes before driving to the rec center. Carlos's pa used to take him to soccer games there when Carlos was little. But, in recent years, Carlos had visited the gym only a couple of times with Toro, who practically lived there. So it wasn't a total surprise when Carlos walked into the weight room and spotted him.

Toro clasped his hand. "Hey, cool hair job."

Carlos glanced in the floor-to-ceiling mirror. "You think it looks okay?"

"Yeah, it looks good. Where'd you get it done?"

"Um, they did it." Carlos nodded toward Sal and Javier as they emerged from the locker room.

Sal spotted Toro and waved cheerily. "Wha's up?"

Toro replied with a nod and whispered to Carlos, "Who's that with him?"

Carlos hesitated. "His, um, boyfriend."

Toro stared at Carlos and lowered his voice. "So he really is . . . *gay*?"

"Yeah. So what? He doesn't mess with me, so why's it such a big deal?"

Toro peered at him, curious-like, as if trying to figure him out.

Carlos quickly changed the subject, knowing Toro loved to show off his knowledge of gym stuff. "What should I work on today?"

Toro led Carlos through a workout, explaining each exercise and spotting for him. But in between sets, he kept darting curious glances at Sal and Javier.

"What's the matter?" Carlos finally asked.

"Nothing," Toro mumbled, but he kept peering over at the guys.

On the ride home from the rec center, Sal glanced over the seat at Carlos and announced, "Javier and I think your friend is gay."

"Huh?" Carlos sat up straight. "Toro? No way! What makes you think that?"

"Gaydar," Javier said matter-of-factly, and Sal elaborated: "It's like a sixth sense. Remember 'I see dead people'? Well, we see gay people."

Carlos shook his head. "You're crazy!" But as they drove home, he thought about how Toro was always looking at muscle mags and hanging out at the rec center. And yet he didn't look or act gay like Sal, or Javier, or the *Queer Eye* guys. And hadn't he had sex with that girl, Leticia? Toro couldn't be gay. No way.

Twenty-Seven

WHEN JAVIER PULLED his car up in front of Carlos's apartment building, Carlos kind of didn't want to say good-bye. "You guys want to hang out for a while?"

Javier and Sal glanced at each other, then Sal turned to Carlos. "Thanks, but . . . Saturday is our date night."

"Oh." Carlos noticed they were holding hands again. "Well . . . um . . . I guess I'll see you later, then."

As he climbed out, Sal rolled down the window. "Remember to cleanse your face before bed!" Javier leaned across Sal and said, "Nice meeting you!"

"Same here." Carlos waved back and watched them drive off, feeling sort of left behind.

In the apartment, Raúl lay on the sofa watching TV. "Hey, new hairstyle, huh? Looks nice."

"Thanks. Can you check my friend's axle if he brings his car to your garage?"

"Sure. No problem. Want to watch the game?"

"What's the score?" Carlos dropped his gym bag and plopped down in the big chair where his pa used to sit.

While they watched the game, Raúl occasionally commented on some play or asked Carlos about school. Carlos liked that Raúl never tried to interfere in his life, unlike his ma's two previous boyfriends.

After the game, Raúl invited Carlos and his ma out to a Chinese restaurant. Apparently, the place was where Raúl took Carlos's ma every Saturday evening, when Carlos was with his pa. All the staff seemed to know them. Across from him in the booth, the two of them sat close together. Once again, Carlos felt left out. He stared down at his shrimp fried rice and wished he had someone special too. He wished he had Roxy.

After dinner, they drove back to the apartment building. As they pulled into the parking lot, his ma asked Carlos, "Did you invite your friends over?"

"No. Why?" He looked out the window. Playboy, Pulga, and Toro were sitting on the steps.

Carlos's ma and Raúl said hi to the boys and went inside, leaving Carlos with them. "'S'up?" Carlos asked.

Playboy stared at Carlos's hair. "Dude, we need to talk to you."

"We heard about you and Sal," Pulga explained. "And his *boyfriend*."

Carlos shot a look at Toro, who lowered his gaze.

"Come on, man," Playboy ordered Carlos. "What's going on?"

Carlos crossed his arms, debating what to do. Obviously, his friends were growing more aggravated. And he was getting tired of hiding. If he told them the truth, they'd probably laugh their asses off. But at least he could stop hiding.

"Okay." Carlos drew a deep breath. "You know that TV show, *Queer Eye for the Straight Guy*? Well, I thought . . ." He wiped his brow and realized he was sweating. "I thought that Sal could help me, so, um, Roxy would notice me."

Playboy's forehead furrowed. Pulga's jaw dropped. Toro gave Carlos a puzzled look. "So you're not gay?" He almost sounded let down.

"No!" Carlos narrowed his eyes at him. "Are *you*?"

Toro's face paled so fast that Carlos wondered if maybe Sal and Javier had been right. *Was* Toro gay?

"Look!" Playboy snapped at Carlos. "We want to know—*are* you?"

Carlos felt his collar tighten. Were his friends listening? Why had he bothered to hide his whole makeover plan, since they weren't going to believe him anyway?

"Yeah!" Carlos said sarcastically. "I'm gay. Don't tell anyone."

"Dude, don't joke like that," Pulga warned him. "Are you?"

"Oh, screw you! Screw all of you." Carlos left them on the steps and went inside, slamming the door behind him.

Twenty-Eight

CARLOS FELT BAD about blowing up at his buds. But hadn't they deserved it?

He tossed his jean jacket onto his dresser and glanced at the photo taped beside his mirror. It was of the four of them, taken at a theme park on Carlos's thirteenth birthday. They'd posed beside a roller coaster, each boy with his fingers raised into "horns" behind another boy's head. Upon seeing the photo, Playboy had dubbed them "Los Horny Boys."

At the time, Carlos's arrival into teenage-hood and the prospect of sex had seemed jam-packed with the promise of thrills and excitement. Now, two and a half years later, it felt like an overrated dud ride, thanks in no small part to his unsupportive pain-in-the-butt friends.

For the rest of the evening, Carlos practiced how to cleanse his face and rub wax into his hair so it spiked like the guys' on TV. The more he looked at his shiny blond highlights, the more he liked them.

Sunday morning he gazed in the mirror, flexing his arms, and thinking his chest might've gotten a little bigger from his workout the previous day. He considered going back to the gym, but his muscles were kind of sore. Besides, he didn't feel like seeing Toro.

Instead, he hung out at home till his ma asked Raúl to go get tortillas, so she could make enchiladas for lunch. Raúl kissed her on the cheek and asked Carlos, "You want to come with me?"

On the trip to the supermarket, Raúl and Carlos mostly talked about cars. But on the drive home, Raúl told Carlos, "You know, I think your ma is a very special lady."

Carlos glanced across the seat at him, wondering why Raúl was telling him that. Were he and his ma planning to get married or something? If they were, why hadn't she told him?

Carlos kept expecting Raúl to say more, but Raúl simply smiled out the truck window. And Carlos felt too awkward to ask more.

As soon as Raúl left after lunch, Carlos confronted his ma. "Are you going to marry him?"

His ma thought a moment before replying, "I'm not sure. We've talked about it, but I don't know yet."

Carlos sputtered, annoyed. He wanted a simple yes or no, not some wussy "I don't know yet." How much longer would she keep squeaking the bedsprings before she made up her mind? And if she did marry Raúl, would they *stay* married?

Carlos retreated to his bedroom and slammed the door. Taking a seat at his computer, he noticed from his buddy list that Playboy, Pulga, and Toro were online. He waited for one of them to IM him. But they didn't. And he was still too angry to IM them.

Instead, he went to Hot-or-Snot and discovered that Roxy had made the day's "Top Picks." Probably every guy in America was e-mailing her. Carlos let out a sigh, wishing *he* had the nerve.

After giving her a ten for the day, he searched for Playboy's profile and gave him a ten too. After all, even though his friends were homophobic *pendejos*, they were still his buds.

Twenty-Nine

Monday morning, Carlos sat in the back row of the bus as usual, but his buds barely said more to him than "'S'up?"

It wasn't till biology class that Toro whispered, "Look, man, I don't care if you *are* gay, we're still friends, okay?"

He tried to shake hands, but Carlos exploded in a whisper, "I'm not gay!"

He refused to let his friends' comments get to him. Besides, he was too busy worrying. Would Roxy notice his hair? Would she like it? If she did, he'd planned exactly what to say: "Thanks. By the way, I saw you on Hot-or-Snot. I gave you a ten."

At lunch, he spotted her and her friends getting ketchup. His heart pounded furiously as he broke into a sweat. Hands trembling, he carried his tray toward her, arriving just as she finished squirting her hot dog.

She turned in his direction. An endless moment passed while she looked at his hair. Then she broke into a smile. "Hey, your hair looks cute." Picking up her tray, she stepped away with her friends, leaving Carlos speechless once again.

And yet a wave of joy flooded through him. True, he hadn't said what he'd planned, but *she* had said more than he'd dared imagine.

He floated toward his table, barely aware of his friends leaning toward him, their eyes wide with curiosity. "What did she say?"

Carlos fell into his chair, still in a daze. "She likes my hair."

"She wants you, dude!" Pulga raised his palm and high-fived him. "So you're really not gay?"

Not that again. "Shut up!"

Pulga responded with a huge smile. "Well, you had me worried, *pendejo*."

"So are you going to e-mail her?" Toro asked.

Only Playboy failed to share their enthusiasm. "Don't waste your time," he told Carlos. "She's a nine-point-eight—out of your league."

"Lay off!" Toro punched Playboy in the shoulder. "That's a crappy thing to say."

Playboy shrugged. "Well, it's true." He turned to Carlos. "You really think Roxy is going to give it up to you just because your queer little boyfriend gives you a fag haircut?"

Pulga rested a hand on Playboy's shoulder. "Hey, ease up, man."

But Carlos wasn't fazed. Sal's encouragement and Roxy's words had fortified his determination. Calmly, he looked Playboy in the eye. "Well . . . at least I'm not snot."

Toro and Pulga gaped at Carlos in astonished admiration. Had he really stood up to Playboy? Then they burst out laughing.

Playboy's eyes narrowed at the three of them. "Screw you, losers!"

But Carlos no longer felt like a loser. He chomped happily on his chicken nuggets, feeling like the luckiest boy at Lone Star High. After lunch he grabbed Sal and told him about Roxy's compliment.

"Cool!" Sal clapped him on the back. "Hey, have you been cleansing your face? It's already looking better."

"No lie?" Carlos rubbed a hand across his chin. "Hey, can you and Javier come over again Saturday?"

"Sure." Sal nodded. "I can. But Javi works on Saturdays. He only took the day off 'cause I asked him to help you."

Carlos hadn't realized that.

"Got to go," Sal said as the bell rang. He started to walk away, then whirled around. "Crap, I forgot to tell you: Harris approved the GSA—thanks to your little ACLU speech. You are *The Man!*"

Carlos beamed. Not only did he no longer feel like a loser, he almost felt like a champion.

Thirty

SATURDAY APPROACHED, AND Carlos debated what to do about visiting his pa. He hadn't really missed seeing him the previous weekend, and he didn't much feel like seeing him the coming weekend. But he'd feel like a creep to tell him that. Instead, he put off saying anything till his pa phoned Friday evening.

"*Mi'jo*, are you coming over this weekend?"

"Um . . ." Carlos gripped the phone, his palms damp. "I'm kind of busy."

"Look . . ." His pa's voice became stern. "I'm not going through this each weekend. You call me when you decide you want to come over again. Okay? *Adios*."

The line cut off. And as Carlos had predicted, he felt like a creep.

Saturday morning when Sal showed up, Carlos asked him, "Can you, um, help me write Roxy an e-mail?"

Even though she surely got a million e-mails a day and would never answer, he'd decided to give it a shot. But in order to send e-mails, the Hot-or-Snot website required a user to first post his or her own profile and photo.

Carlos and Sal worked on his DESCRIPTION. It started out easy: *Six feet tall, brown hair, brown eyes* . . . But then he got stuck. "What else?"

"'Nice smile,'" Sal suggested.

"You don't think it's too yellow and dingy?"

Actually, it did seem a little brighter since he'd cut out cola drinks like Sal had recommended and started brushing twice a day like he was supposed to.

"Type it," Sal ordered, and Carlos did. Then Sal suggested, "'Hot bod.'"

"No way!" Carlos protested. "I don't have a hot bod."

"Javi and I think so. And we're gay. We should know."

"Shut up." Carlos squirmed in his chair, feeling weird about his friends checking out his body. "I can't put 'hot bod.' It sounds conceited."

Sal gave a sigh. "Then list some personality stuff—things you like about yourself."

Carlos thought for moment, but it was easier for him to think about the things he *didn't* like about himself. "Um . . . I don't know. Like what?"

Sal rolled his eyes. "You're honest . . ."

"Not always," Carlos mumbled.

"Dude!" Sal scolded. "What's with your self-image issues? You've got to learn to like yourself. Nobody's perfect. You're *mostly* honest, aren't you?"

"Yeah." Carlos shrugged. "I guess."

"Then type it."

As Carlos typed, Sal dictated: "You're down-to-earth . . . easygoing . . . sweet, nice . . . shy, funny . . . good sense of humor . . . intelligent . . ."

"I can't put all that," Carlos protested. But Sal ordered: "Type!"

Carlos's LIKES list came easier: *Hanging out with friends, video (especially car racing) games, music (Tejano, pop, Latin pop, Los Lonely Boys), working out (just starting).*

His DISLIKES were even more fun: *Fakes, phonies, jerks, cabbage, loud motorcycles, cold weather . . .* Suddenly Carlos thought of one other major dislike: *Bigoted homophobes (and no, I'm not gay, but some of my friends are).*

Sal gently leaned into him. "Hey, thanks, man."

"No problem." Carlos avoided glancing at him, afraid Sal would give him that annoying tender look again.

"By the way," Sal said. "We're putting up flyers next week about the GSA. Okay?"

"Yeah," Carlos replied, not paying much attention. "Now, can you take a picture of me?" He handed Sal his camera. "Where should I stand?"

Sal scanned the room. "Next to the praying mantis."

They moved the bed aside and Carlos stood beside the shiny green insect in its clear frame. Sal peered at the camera screen. "Now, lift up your shirt."

"You crazy?" Carlos clutched his shirt. "I can't do that. No way. I don't want everybody on the planet to see my stomach."

"Stop saying 'I can't!' Just say 'Yes!' Tell the world, 'I'm hot, damn it!'"

Carlos shook his head. "Yeah, right."

"I'm waaaiting . . ." Sal held the camera steady.

Carlos moaned a sigh, forced a big smile, and yanked his shirt up for a split second. In that instant, the flash went off.

Carlos hurried over to view the image. He usually hated photos of himself, but surprisingly, he didn't totally hate this one. "You think it's okay?"

"It's hot!" Sal assured him as they uploaded the pic onto Hot-or-Snot.

The next step was to wait for the site moderator's approval. In the meantime, Carlos asked Sal's help to compose the message to Roxy. "Okay, so what should I say?"

"Well, what do you want to say?"

"I don't know. Every time I see her I lose my voice and break into a sweat. She probably thinks I'm a mute with a perspiration problem. Not to mention, my mind goes straight to her boobs."

Sal grimaced. "Why are straight guys so obsessed with breasts?"

"Well . . ." Carlos thought for a moment. "Because boobs are cool."

"Yeah, whatever." Sal returned to the task at hand. "Okay, let's start with 'Dear Roxy . . . You probably think of me as Ketchup Guy . . .'"

Carlos's fingers hovered over the keyboard. "Isn't that kind of a geeky thing to say?"

"Nah. It's self-deprecating humor. Girls love that."

It never stopped amazing Carlos how much Sal knew about girls. Maybe that's why gay guys existed: to help straight guys figure out women. While pondering that, he received an e-mail notifying him that his profile was approved. It made him nervously want to scrap the whole idea, but Sal continued dictating. "How about saying, 'I like you and I'd like to get to know you better'?"

"Are you nuts?" Carlos shook his head. "I can't tell her I like her!"

"Why not? You do, don't you?"

"Yeah, but I can't tell her that. What if she thinks I'm gross?"

"Why would she think you're gross?"

"Because . . ." Carlos's voice trailed off. He was too embarrassed to admit that sometimes *he* thought he was gross.

"Look," Sal said, "did you ever stop to consider that maybe *she* likes *you,* too?"

Carlos turned silent, catapulted by the idea into boob-land.

"Okay," Sal told him. "How about if, instead, you write 'I think you're cute'?"

"But she's not just cute," Carlos griped. "She's beautiful."

"All right," Sal amended. "Then tell her: 'I think you're beautiful.'"

"Nah." Carlos resumed typing. "Let's stick with 'I think you're cute,' but let's skip that 'know you better' stuff. It sounds weird. How about 'I'd like to chat with you sometime . . . I mean, if you'd like to. My screen name is LonelyBoy78703.'" He turned to Sal. "Does that sound all right?"

"It sounds great, Casanova."

But Carlos wasn't convinced. "I'm not going to send this." He moved the cursor to the delete button.

"Don't you dare!" Sal grabbed his hand, shooting him a piercing look. "Just send it!"

"Okay, okay!" Carlos scowled back at him. "Let go of me!" He shook off Sal's hand and clicked send, even though he was sure Roxy would never answer.

And yet, a secret thrill coursed through him. What if she did?

Thirty-One

AFTER SENDING ROXY the e-mail, Carlos and Sal surfed the web till Carlos began getting hungry. His ma was busy tending to sewing clients, so he asked Sal, "You hungry? Why don't you teach me to make something for lunch?"

That seemed like the next logical step in his makeover.

Sal shook his head. "I don't know how to cook."

Carlos blinked in surprise. "The *Queer Eye* guys do."

"So? Get over it. There are five of them and only one of me. I'm not Super Gay."

Carlos felt a little let down—and still hungry. "Well, do you like grilled cheese? That's the only thing I know how to make. Besides cereal."

"Grilled cheese is fine. You can teach *me* something for a change."

"All right." Carlos nodded proudly.

In the kitchen, he proceeded to explain: "First, you butter the bread. That gives it the good flavor. Then you set the stove burner on low, so the cheese will melt slow and the bread won't burn. I cook it open-face and cover the skillet with a lid to help the cheese melt. Then you put the other slice of bread on top and flip it over."

As Carlos demonstrated his technique, Raúl arrived for his Saturday visit. "What are you guys making? It smells great."

"Grilled cheese. You want one?"

"Sure!" Raúl replied as Sal nudged Carlos to introduce them.

After lunch, the two boys returned to Carlos's room, and Sal commented, "Your ma's boyfriend seems nice."

"He's okay. I guess." Carlos sat down at his computer, not wanting to talk about Raúl.

"Hey." Sal spun Carlos's chair around. "What's going on? I can always tell when there's something you're not telling me. You get that constipated look on your face."

Carlos clenched his jaw, trying to keep from telling Sal about how he could hear his ma and Raúl. He'd never talked about that to anyone, not even his buds. But now the words suddenly seemed to jab at his throat, wanting to come out.

"It's just . . ." Carlos said in a low voice, glancing toward the open doorway. "He stays over and . . . I can hear them."

"*Hear* them?" Sal whispered. "Hear them *what*?"

"You know . . ." Carlos scowled. "*Hear*. Them."

"You mean sex?" Sal leaned in closer. "You listen to your mom having sex?"

"Hey, shut up!" Carlos ran to close his bedroom door, mortified his ma or Raúl might've heard. "I don't *listen* to her. I can just hear them through the wall."

"Dude, that's gross!" Sal made a face. "Have you told her?"

Carlos plunked into the desk chair and crossed his arms. "I can't tell her that."

"Why not? Do you enjoy hearing her?"

"You're sick!" Carlos snapped, wishing he hadn't told Sal anything.

"Dude . . ." Sal said more softly. "If you want people to change, you've got to change first. It's like that Gandhi quote in the library: 'Be the change you wish to see in the world.' If you keep bottling stuff up inside, one of these days you're going to explode."

Carlos did feel ready to explode. At least by telling Sal about his ma, Carlos felt relieved of hiding the secret. But now he had a new worry. "Promise you won't tell anyone about this?"

"Yeah, right. Who am I going to tell? You're the one who needs to tell—*your mom!*"

No way, Carlos thought. Telling Sal had been hard enough. Not wanting to think about it, he spun his chair around to the computer to check if maybe, by some remote chance, he could possibly have gotten an e-mail from Roxy.

But his mailbox was empty. He'd known she wouldn't write back. He crossed his arms and slumped down in his chair.

Sal must've sensed his disappointment. "Give her a chance, for God's sake!"

Carlos stared at his empty mailbox till Sal asked, "You want to go work out?"

Better than waiting for mail that's never going to come, Carlos thought.

When the two boys got to the rec center, Toro was there again. At first he appeared noticeably uneasy, averting his eyes and popping his knuckles.

But as Sal asked for help with exercises, Toro seemed to relax . . . until Sal asked, "Will you help us start our GSA?"

"Um . . ." Toro paled as if about to pass out—and it wasn't from the exercise. "I'm not gay." He left Carlos and Sal to work out on their own after that.

Later, as they were heading home, Sal whispered to Carlos, "He is *definitely* gay."

"Shut up," Carlos told him, although he wondered why Toro had gotten so flustered.

Later that afternoon, Sal left for his weekly date with Javier, and Carlos spent another boring Saturday night eating Chinese food with his ma and Raúl.

Once they returned home, he put on his headphones and cranked up the music while checking to see if there was any message from GlitterGirl Roxy. There still wasn't. But to Carlos's amazement, his own profile rating remained well above "snot" level. Delighted, he surfed the web, singing to his music.

He was downloading a new song when, abruptly, an IM popped onto his screen. He glanced at the name and nearly sprang out of his chair. It was from GlitterGirl.

Thirty-Two

As Carlos stared at Roxy's IM, a torrent of sweat accumulated on his face. Was he seeing things? The message had to be a hoax. Maybe it was from Sal, teasing him. Hand trembling, Carlos clicked on the message.

GlitterGirl: Wassup? So, ur Ketchup Guy?

Carlos swallowed hard, trying to quench his suddenly parched throat. Out of all the e-mails Roxy received, why had she responded to his? More to the point, now what was he supposed to say? He mustered all his brainpower and replied, *Yeah. Hi.*

He hit send and stared at the screen, unblinking, as his mind uncontrollably conjured boobs.

After what seemed like centuries, a new GlitterGirl IM appeared: *I'm soooo bored. What r u up 2?*

Now Carlos was convinced this had to be a hoax. How could the finest babe at Lone Star High possibly be bored? Just having those boobs ruled out any chance of boredom. And why was she asking him so many questions?

Nothing, he typed back shakily. *Bored too.*

He hit send and waited, staring at the computer, wishing he'd asked her a question so she'd respond. And yet, she replied anyway: *Ur bored too? Guess that makes 2 of us. Hmm . . .* ☺

Carlos carefully studied the text, tracing his finger across the screen, trying to decipher its meaning. What did she mean by "Hmm?" And what did her wink mean?

Carlos yanked off his headphones and sprang from his chair, unable to sit still. He needed to reply, but what should he say? He paced the room, trying to think, but his mind had turned to boob-mush.

Another IM popped onto the computer screen: *U still there? Got2go. L8erz.*

Carlos leaned over the monitor as his heart slid down his chest and into his feet. *Laterz,* he quickly typed, adding, *Thanks.* He wasn't sure why he added that, except Sal was always harping on him to.

After waiting at the computer an hour, just in case Roxy sent another IM, Carlos finally got up from the desk. As he got ready for bed, his legs felt a little wobbly. With her message, Roxy had rocked his world. How could he possibly have told her he was bored? He'd never felt more excited in his entire life.

Thirty-Three

MONDAY MORNING, CARLOS boarded his bus and stared Playboy directly in the eye. "Guess who IM-ed me? Roxy."

"Yeah, right," Playboy scoffed. "In your dreams."

"Your *wet* dreams." Pulga grinned.

"Don't believe me." Carlos gave a shrug. "I don't care."

"Did she really?" Toro asked. "You going to hook up with her?"

"I haven't decided." Carlos glanced out the window, trying to play it cool.

But, as if not to be outdone, Playboy hijacked the conversation. "You guys won't believe the new chick who messaged me last night."

"Is she under thirty?" Pulga asked.

"Check this out, smart ass." Playboy showed the guys her photo on his cell phone. "Her user name is BadAssGirl."

The multi-earringed girl leaned toward the camera, her tongue licking her blood-red lips. A swath of black hair hung over one eye as her hand pulled up her ripped T-shirt. Her flat, tiny stomach revealed a gleaming belly-button ring and a tattooed heart etched with the word DANGGER.

"That's not how you spell 'danger'," Carlos observed.

"I'm not asking her to a spelling bee." Playboy gazed at the mini-screen. "Her profile says, 'I'm the girl you love to hate. Your best dream and worst nightmare. Hot as fire but sweet as rain. Try me . . . if you dare.' Doesn't she sound crazy?"

To Carlos, she did sound crazy—kind of psycho, to be precise. But he didn't want to rain on Playboy's parade. Besides, his thoughts remained preoccupied with another girl: the one who had messaged him over a thousand other guys.

All that morning, Carlos's heart pounded with the anticipation of seeing her. When he finally spotted Roxy at lunchtime, a smile exploded across his face. He lifted a trembling hand, excitedly waving.

Roxy glanced over and sort of waved back with her fork, but she continued talking to her friends.

"Dude, don't act so desperate!" Playboy brought Carlos's hand down. "Chill out."

Carlos dropped his hand to the table and his heart crashed back to earth. He hadn't meant to act desperate; he was just so excited. How could he hide that?

He twirled his spaghetti, continuing to steal glances at Roxy, wondering if he'd ruined his chances of dating her because of his overly exuberant wave. He only half listened to Pulga bemoan his latest frustration with Carlotta:

"She's pissed because I didn't get her a birthday present. So I told her, 'Look, we're not dating! Why can't we just have fun?' She's a lot of fun till she starts the dating crap."

"Then why don't you just date her?" Toro asked, sipping his juice.

"No way! It's too embarrassing. We'd look ridiculous together—little me and tall her. At least this way she doesn't go around blabbing that we're hooking up."

Carlos gazed across the lunchroom, wondering if Roxy were embarrassed by *him*. Was that why she'd barely waved to him?

During the next couple of days, each time he glimpsed Roxy he nearly burst through his skin from excitement. But he fought to control his exuberance, coolly nodding, "'S'up?"

Yet, when he got home, alone in his room, he stared at his computer screen for hours, wishing another IM from Roxy would appear.

Thirty-Four

WHEN CARLOS PHONED Sal the news of Roxy's IM, the response was way different from Carlos's buds: "Who loves you, baby? I told you, you're hot."

Carlos squirmed at the comment, and yet for the first time he wondered, *Could it possibly be true?* Was he hot? But then, why did Roxy barely give him a fork-wave at lunch?

"Hey, listen up!" Sal continued. "On Wednesday we're putting up GSA posters after school, okay?"

"Huh?" Carlos asked, his mind still glued to thoughts of Roxy.

"GSA posters! Wednesday. After school. Don't forget. *Okay?*"

Fortunately, he reminded Carlos during lunch on Wednesday. "We're meeting in the library. Mr. Quiñones agreed to be our advisor."

"Advisor? For what?"

"The GSA!" He tapped Carlos's head. "*Remember?*"

When the last bell rang, Carlos headed to the meeting. He'd stopped making excuses to his buds; he merely didn't show up for his bus.

In the library, Mr. Quiñones, the school's head librarian, was at the front counter, sorting books. Everyone heard rumors that he was gay, for no clear reason. He was a soft-spoken, easygoing guy—tall, thin, and kind of quirky. He'd posted signs with quotations from famous dead guys all around the library. Some were serious, like:

This above all:
To thine own self be true
—William Shakespeare

Other quotes were sort of funny, like:

To love oneself is the beginning
of a lifelong romance
—Oscar Wilde

"Oh, hi, Carlos." Mr. Quiñones smiled from the checkout counter. "I was glad to hear from Sal you'll be in the GSA."

"But I'm not gay," Carlos blurted out.

Mr. Quiñones's smile grew even wider. "I never imagined you were."

Yeah, right, Carlos thought.

From a table near the window Sal called to Carlos, "We're back here!"

Freaky Vicky sat beside him. Today she looked as though she'd stepped out of *That '70s Show,* wearing a psychedelic tie-dyed T-shirt, cloth headband, and flowers painted on her cheeks. Apparently, she'd also brought Day-Glo poster paper to make the GSA signs.

Espie showed up wearing her orange hoodie and smiled at Carlos. "Hi. I like your highlights."

"Um, thanks." Little beads of sweat erupted on Carlos's forehead. At least Espie's zipped-up hoodie helped keep his mind off what her boobs might be like. He tried convincing himself that beneath her baggy sweatshirt, she was probably flat as a pancake.

"Sal and his boyfriend did them."

"Really?" Espie gazed at him from beneath her hood. "Maybe I should ask them to do my hair."

"Um, yeah, you should." Carlos immediately worried that sounded wrong. "I mean, not that your hair looks bad now—at least from what I can see."

But that sounded wrong too. "I mean, you've probably got nice hair I can't see, too."

Great, now he sounded like a perv. "I don't mean—you know—down *there*. I mean on your head. I just can't see it."

By some miracle, Espie didn't seem to take offense at his blithering. Instead, she pulled her hood down to her shoulders, revealing her silky brown hair. "You don't think it's too frizzy? I've never liked it."

"Um, it's pretty," Carlos uttered before being struck numb again.

Espie unzipped her hoodie, revealing that she wasn't flat as a pancake. Her boobs weren't Roxy spectacular, but they were definitely nice.

"Thanks." She extended a bag of gummy bears in her hand. "You want one?"

Apparently, she thought Carlos was staring down at her candy. "I brought them for everyone."

"Um, thanks." Carlos stuffed a handful of gummies into his mouth, hoping they would help him calm down and shut up.

"Hi!" Carlotta greeted everyone, carrying masking tape and magic markers. With her arrival, the group set to work, making a dozen posters with slogans like:

TIRED OF HOMOHOBIA?
HELP US FIGHT IT

And:

GAY IS OKAY!
COME OUT FOR THE GSA

When they were done, Sal divided them up to post the signs. "I'll do the cafeteria. Espie and Vicky, you do the north hall. Carlos and Carlotta, you do the east hall."

Carlos kind of wished he could've gone with Espie, but it was probably best that he didn't, so he wouldn't blather all sorts of stupidness again.

"I tried to get Pulga to help us," Carlotta informed Carlos as they walked down the empty hallway, "but he said, 'No way.'" She handed Carlos the tape while she put up a poster. "Can I ask you something? What does he say about me?"

Carlos fumbled with the tape, dropping it. "Um, what do you mean?"

"I mean . . ." Carlotta picked up the tape and handed it to him again. "Sometimes I think he just wants me for my body."

She definitely had quite a length of body—even taller than Carlos, her boobs currently just below his nose. Carlos forced himself to look up from the breasts to her face—a pretty face, with big, brown giraffe-like eyes, long lashes, and a warm, friendly smile.

"Tell me the truth." Carlotta pushed a strand of hair away from her forehead. "Does he really like me?"

Carlos watched her eyes puddle up. "Um, yeah, he likes you."

"Then why won't he date me?" She wiped her cheek.

"I don't know," Carlos said softly. He'd always thought she was nice. Now he felt bad for her—and helpless that he didn't know how to comfort her.

As they finished putting up posters, he thought that Sal's GSA was turning out to be more than he'd bargained for.

Thirty-Five

CARLOS BROODED ALL afternoon. That evening, Raúl came over for his midweek visit. As usual, after dinner and TV, Carlos's ma and Raúl went to bed. And Carlos went to his computer, put his headphones on, and cranked the music full blast so he wouldn't hear them.

Ever since he'd told Sal about all that, he'd felt a sense of relief. But he'd also started to feel angry—not only with his ma and Raúl, but at himself for not speaking up about it. Maybe Sal was right: He should talk to his ma. But how?

He tried to take his mind off the whole thing by playing his Master Kick Butt computer game, punching and kicking his adversaries. Just as he faced a new opponent, an IM popped onto the screen. Startled, Carlos lost control of his player, who got hit, kicked down, and tossed off a cliff.

But Carlos didn't care. The IM was from GlitterGirl Roxy, asking, *Wassup?*

Thirty-Six

CARLOS STARED AT Roxy's IM, wide-eyed and unblinking, as a million questions jammed his brain. Why had she suddenly written him again? Especially after practically ignoring him at school? Was she interested in him after all?

His heart pumped optimism and his mind ballooned with boobs. Roxy had thought of him, totally without his prompting. He yanked his headphones off and leaped up from his chair as he tried to figure out: What should he respond?

Abruptly, he sat down again. *Nothing's up here. Sup with u?*

He hit send and awaited her response, wiping the sudden waterfall of sweat pouring off his forehead.

Nothing at all, Roxy IM-ed back. *Bored . . . bored . . . booored!!! My mom's working late and my little bro's in bed so I can't go out. What about u?*

Carlos scratched his leg, considering how to interpret her question. Was she asking if he could go out? No, that couldn't possibly be it. She must be asking about his ma.

My ma's gone to bed, Carlos explained, but left out mentioning Raúl. *I don't have any bros or sis's.*

Lucky u, Roxy answered back. *What about ur dad?*

Carlos typed: *My folks split up.*

Roxy: *Mine too.*

Sorry.

No big deal.

Carlos stared at her message, trying to figure out what to say next. Ideally, he'd keep things rolling with something clever and funny. But nothing came to mind. Their conversation had screeched to a dismal halt. Carlos slumped in his chair, disappointed yet also amazed that he'd written as much as he had. Sal would be proud of him.

Suddenly Roxy IM-ed again: *So what r u up to tonite?*

Carlos sat up with renewed confusion. Hadn't he already told her he wasn't doing anything?

Not much, he reiterated, wondering how many times they could cover the same territory. He never expected what Roxy sent next: *Ur cute. U wanna come over?*

Carlos read the message three times. It had to be a joke. Could the girl of his dreams truly be inviting him to her house? Fantasies collided inside his brain, exploding in images of boobs, lips, kisses, and hands . . .

Another IM appeared on his screen: *Hellooooo!!! R U THERE???*

Carlos stared at the message, thinking *I can't do this.*

But wasn't this what he'd always wished for? A voice in his mind sneered, *Loser!* as he brought his fists to his forehead, pounding it. But then a new encouraging voice gently whispered inside his brain: *Stop saying, 'I can't!' Just say 'Yes!'*

The words rang so clearly that Carlos whirled around, half expecting to see Sal. But no one was there. He turned back to the computer, his hands nearly shaking off the keyboard as he typed: *U want me 2 come over?*

He hit send and waited breathless for Roxy's answer.

It came back fast: *Yeah. U wanna?*

One by one, Carlos typed what seemed like the most important three letters of his entire life: *Yes.*

Then he drew an enormous breath and hit send.

Thirty-Seven

AN INSTANT LATER, Roxy IM-ed Carlos her street address, adding: *Hurry! I'm not supposed to have guys over. My mom gets home @ 12.*

Carlos remained in his chair, trying to make his heart slow down. What if Roxy's mom came home early? But it was barely ten o'clock. Besides, the vision of Roxy's boobs quickly pushed aside fear of her mom. His bigger concern was, what if Roxy actually wanted to make out? Would she realize he was the only fifteen-year-old who'd never French-kissed?

The image of her lips beckoned just beyond reach. Carlos desperately needed to bolster his courage. But how?

He grabbed the phone and called Sal. But Sal didn't answer. Carlos was on his own.

His legs wobbled as he got up and walked to the mirror. At least his crater face had cleared some—quite a bit, actually. His teeth were a little whiter. And hadn't Roxy said his hair looked cute? Maybe Sal was right: Maybe he wasn't as gross-looking as he'd thought.

His hands trembled as he carefully sprayed fresh deodorant and changed into the black shirt he'd bought with Sal. He tucked it into his patchwork jeans and SEXY belt buckle. Then he pulled on his denim jacket and glanced in the mirror again, taking a good, hard look at himself.

He started to say something, but stopped. Then he forced himself. Even though barely a whisper, he said it aloud: "I'm hot, damn it."

Flushing bright red, he quickly left the room.

As Carlos padded down the carpeted hallway, he debated telling his ma he was going out. Behind her bedroom door, it was quiet. Why wake her just to have her ask a bunch of questions? Besides, Raúl was with her. And what if she told Carlos he couldn't go out? What would he tell Roxy? He didn't want her to think he was a baby.

Better to leave a note. That way, in the unlikely event his ma did notice he was gone, at least she wouldn't worry to death. But did he really want to tell her he was going to a girl's house? He decided to say he was going to Sal's.

After placing the note on the kitchen table, Carlos tiptoed across the darkened living room and slipped out the front door into the cool, dark night. Upon reaching the sidewalk, he stepped quickly toward Roxy's. Although he didn't want to arrive sweaty and stinky, it took all his willpower to keep himself from sprinting.

Thirty-Eight

ROXY LIVED ON the third floor of a Spanish-style pink stucco building only six blocks from Carlos, even though they took different buses. His hand shook as he tapped her apartment door knocker, half expecting Sal or Playboy to jump out, yelling, "Fooled you!"

But when the door opened, Carlos blinked in disbelief. There stood Roxy, live and in person.

She gave Carlos a friendly little greeting smile while talking into her cell phone: "Uh-huh . . . yeah . . . I know what you mean."

Carlos's gaze moved to her necklace, from which a tiny gold heart dangled into the cleavage of her scoop-neck T-shirt.

"He told you he wanted *what*?" She continued talking into the phone. "You're kidding . . . I say dump him." She motioned Carlos in toward the living room sofa. The TV was on, broadcasting a tampon commercial.

"Sorry about that," Roxy said, hanging up her phone. "Sit down. You want a Diet Sprite?"

"Um, sure," Carlos replied, his throat parched from nervousness. He watched her glide barefoot toward the kitchen, her teeny, tight black nylon shorts showing off her long, smooth legs. When she'd disappeared, he sat down and caught his breath.

The place seemed messier than he would've expected. *Teen People* and *telenovela* magazines lay open on the coffee table, and little kids' toys were scattered around the worn carpet. Prior to Sal, Carlos never would've noticed messiness. Now, he neatly arranged the magazines on the table to help calm his nerves.

When Roxy came back and handed him his drink, he remembered to tell her, "Thanks."

"You're welcome." She slid onto the sofa next to him as the TV program resumed: *Queer Eye*.

Carlos nearly choked on his drink. The coincidence was way too freaky. Playboy and Pulga had to be spying from the next room, laughing their butts off.

"Are you okay?" Roxy patted Carlos's back to soothe his coughing.

"I'm fine," he wheezed, gulping his drink.

Roxy extended the remote control to turn the volume up. "I think fags are so funny. Did you hear they're starting a homo club at school?"

Carlos winced. "Um, it's actually a Gay-Straight Alliance."

"Oh." Roxy peered silently at him, her gaze moving to his blond highlights. "You're not gay, are you?"

"No! No, no."

"I mean, tell me if you are."

"No!" Carlos gave his head a vigorous shake. "I'm not."

Roxy's brow relaxed as the corner of her lips curved into a little smile. "That's good."

She turned to the TV, where the gays were teaching the straight guy to make spiced nuts in a skillet, with brown sugar, cinnamon, cloves, and allspice.

A mix of emotions stirred in Carlos. He'd never expected the girl of his dreams to use terms like "fag" and "homo." Granted, in his fantasies she barely spoke as she tore away his pants and threw herself at him.

Now, she lifted her bare legs onto the coffee table and crossed her ankles. In the glow of the TV, she radiated a vision of beauty, from her sparkling pink toenails to the shimmering gold heart dangling between her breasts.

"Why are you staring at me?" she asked out of the corner of her mouth.

Carlos's face flared so hot he could've fried an egg on it. "Um . . . your eyes are really nice."

"Thanks. But my eyes are up here."

"Um, yeah. Sorry." But as Carlos forced his gaze to the TV, the image of Roxy's legs and cleavage stayed emblazoned in his mind.

The show reached the point where the gay guys revealed to the straight dude his redecorated apartment. Roxy excitedly uncrossed her ankles, and in the process laid her hand beside Carlos. "I love this part!"

Carlos's attention remained focused on her hand. Did she expect him to take hold of it? What if she yanked it away, shouting, "Dude! What the hell do you think you're doing? I only invited you to hang out. Get out of here! Now!"

Then again, what if she thought he was a lug for not making a move? He sat stiffly, sweat streaming down his back. What to do? He didn't want to make the wrong move. But what was the right move?

On TV, the gay guys prepared to unveil the new, improved straight guy to his girlfriend. Without warning, Roxy grabbed hold of Carlos's hand. He jumped. And Roxy giggled. "What's the matter?"

"Nothing." He cleared his throat and gripped her hand in return, a little fearful she might pull it away again. But was he clutching it too tight? Quickly, he loosened his grip, and realized how clammy his palm was. Would she be grossed out?

If she was, she didn't show it. Without turning from the TV, Carlos stole a glance at her lips. Now that she'd taken hold of his hand, firmly establishing they were more than friends, the next logical step was to kiss. But how? Was he supposed to simply lean over and plop his tongue into her mouth? Good thing that Sal had made him start to brush and floss regularly.

On TV the girlfriend thanked the gay guys for making over her boyfriend. It made Carlos wonder what advice Sal would give him, kissing-wise. They'd never talked about stuff like that, nor did the guys on TV. But, knowing Sal, he'd probably say something like, "Ask first."

And yet, in movies the guy never asked the girl. He simply looked meaningfully into her eyes.

Carlos turned to Roxy. He tried to give her what he thought was a meaningful look.

"Yeah?" she said, still watching the TV.

"Um . . ." He took a deep breath, his throat tightening over it, and whispered, "Can I kiss you?"

He held his breath, expecting the worst.

"Wait till the commercial," Roxy replied. "I want to see the ending."

Carlos turned back to the TV, amazed. Roxy had neither laughed nor screamed at him. So, what would happen once the commercial came? Was she expecting a mouth-kiss? He should have clarified that.

The program ended and Roxy turned to Carlos. "Okay." Her eyebrows lifted expectantly, her lips parted slightly, and to Carlos's immense relief, it was obvious what kind of kiss she wanted.

Keeping his eyes open so as not to screw up, he leaned toward her. His lips gently came to rest on hers, and a thousand microscopic nerve endings quivered. Tasting her sweetness, his soul quaked too. He let his eyes close and lost himself in time, wishing their kiss could last forever.

A moment later, he came back with a jolt. How much time had elapsed? He didn't want to seem greedy. Quickly, he pulled away.

"Why are you stopping?" Roxy whispered. "Don't stop!"

"Sorry." Carlos returned his face to hers, more confident now, feeling like he was getting the hang of it. And when she tapped her tongue against his, it seemed like the most natural thing on earth.

As their lips pressed and parted, their breaths came harder, chests rising and falling. And Carlos became keenly aware of Roxy's breasts squishing against him. He tried to pull away, fearing she might think he was trying to cop a feel. But the breasts seemed to chase after him.

Suddenly, Roxy pulled her mouth away and gasped, "Do you want to see them?"

Carlos blinked, a little dazed. This was too much like a scene from his fantasies to be true. So he simply said, "Um, okay."

Thirty-Nine

ROXY LEANED BACK on the couch, her boobs waiting beneath the scoop-neck T-shirt.

Except . . . Carlos wasn't exactly sure how to proceed. Even though his buds and he had spent endless hours extolling the marvels of breasts, they'd never discussed the specifics of precisely what to do if a girl willingly volunteered them.

As if understanding Carlos's plight, Roxy took hold of his hand.

She rested his quivering palm on her T-shirt and he rocketed into ecstasy. Every nerve of each fingertip leaped with joy as he gently, uncertainly stroked. He hadn't expected the breast to feel so supple and yet firm.

Roxy closed her eyes, smiling peacefully until, after a while, she lowered her voice as if telling a secret: "You can touch the other one too, you know."

"Um, sorry." Carlos immediately shifted his hand. He hadn't meant to snub the other boob. Determined not to repeat his blunder, he now alternated, giving each equal time.

Abruptly, Roxy's cell phone rang. Carlos jumped with a start, yanking his hand away from her chest.

"Ugh!" Roxy groaned, grabbing the phone. She glanced at the caller ID and answered, "Did you tell him? What did he say?"

While pressing the phone to her ear, Roxy reached for Carlos's hand and laid it on top of her breasts again.

Who is she talking to? Carlos wondered.

"Don't worry about that," she spoke into the phone. "Oral is oral, it's not sex. It's like kissing—except you're kissing something else."

She darted a devilish glance at Carlos and said to whomever she was talking, "Listen, I've got to go. I'll call you later and tell you about it, okay?"

What exactly will you tell them later? Carlos wondered as Roxy hung up. He wanted to ask, except she suddenly took hold of his wrist and slid his hand underneath her shirt.

Shit, she's bra-less! As his fingertips touched her naked skin, his heart slammed against his chest. He was touching Roxy Rodriguez's breasts—skin on skin. Had anyone known greater joy? He wanted to borrow the phone and call his own friends.

Except, he would like to see the breasts first. Fingers quavering, he nudged Roxy's T-shirt up. She good-naturedly aided him along, guiding him like an angel with perky breasts.

"Kiss them," she whispered.

Carlos gazed up. "Huh?"

"Kiss them."

Carlos gulped, slightly terrified. But how could he refuse? Leaning forward, he gently pressed his lips onto her breast. Roxy gave a soft moan.

Carlos glanced up to make sure he hadn't hurt her. But her face displayed no sign of pain. With increasing agility, he planted a tender kiss on her other breast.

Roxy squirmed and moaned, her flat, smooth stomach arching beneath him.

Feeling nearly like a pro now, Carlos began moving his mouth slowly from one breast to another, lightly brushing his lips across the pliant skin till Roxy suddenly gasped.

"Are you okay?" Carlos quickly pulled away.

In response, she wrapped her arms around his shoulders and head, pressing his face so tight against her breasts that he could hardly breathe. But he didn't mind. He'd gladly have given up breathing for the rest of his life.

Forty

Unfortunately, a few minutes later Roxy pulled her T-shirt down over her boobs, closing up shop. "That's enough. My mom will be home soon."

Carlos slumped back on the sofa, dazed.

"Hey!" Roxy giggled, shaking his shoulder. "What are you doing? Get up!"

"Huh?" Carlos rubbed his eyes, feeling as though he were waking from a dream.

"Come on!" Roxy stood up, tugging on his arm. "You've got to go. It's almost midnight. I don't want to get in trouble."

"Okay." Carlos stumbled to his feet, oblivious to the tent in his pants—till Roxy burst into laughter, exclaiming, "Boys!"

Carlos blushed, wishing he could hide beneath the couch, but Roxy was already hustling him across the room.

At the door, he politely said, "Thanks," like Sal had taught him.

Roxy grinned, tracing a finger gently across his cheek, and told him, "You're funny."

Carlos hadn't meant to be funny. As he practically soared toward home, bounding over curbs and leaping over fire hydrants, his entire body hummed with energy. This had been the best evening of his life.

But as he glanced up toward the living room window of his apartment, he abruptly slammed to a halt. Why was the light on?

Fearing the worst, he tiptoed up the staircase. As he fished out his keys, they fell from his trembling hands and jingled to the floor.

Carlos stooped to retrieve them. The front door opened. A pair of pink slippers appeared. Carlos gazed up. Above him towered his ma, her arms crossed, her dark eyes blazing. "Where were you?"

"Um . . ." Carlos gathered himself up. He once again stood much taller than his ma, and slinked past her and Raúl into the living room, wondering what excuse he could give. "I left a note. Didn't you see it?"

His ma gave him a sharp look. "It said you were at Sal's. But Sal phoned and said you weren't with him."

Carlos glanced down at the carpet. Why had Sal phoned, tonight of all nights?

"Tell me the truth!" his ma demanded. "You're an hour past your curfew."

Carlos clutched the keys in his hand. "Um, I started to go to Sal's, but then I went to another friend's instead. That's all."

"*What* friend?" his ma persisted.

"Um . . . a new friend."

"Carlos, I want to know who your friends are. What's his name?"

Carlos balled his fist around the keys, shoving them into his pocket. "Um, it's a girl."

"A *girl*?" His ma's voice rose with surprise. "What were you doing with a girl?"

Inside Carlos's brain, Roxy's boobs magically appeared. "Nothing. We weren't doing anything."

"You were doing *something*," his ma insisted, pushing the hair from her face.

Her self-righteous tone ticked him off. "What do you *think* we were doing?"

"Maybe," Raúl intervened, "you two should talk this out tomorrow—when you're both calmer?"

Carlos and his ma both glared at him. Then she whirled back toward Carlos, stabbing her finger in the air. "You'd better not get any girl in trouble! You're not a child anymore. Now go to your room!"

You sound ridiculous, he thought. Maybe she thought so too, because she clutched her robe tightly around herself and marched into her own room.

Raúl gave Carlos an odd, conspiring look and patted him on the shoulder. "You should get some sleep."

Carlos was left standing on his own, feeling strangely grown-up and a little nervous. Even though his ma had scolded him like a kid, she'd acknowledged he wasn't one. *Would* he accidentally get Roxy in trouble?

Inside his room, he peeled off his clothes, feeling slightly out of control: for lying to his ma, for sneaking off, for doing the stuff he'd done with Roxy. And yet, as he climbed into bed and recalled their kisses, warm feelings flowed over him again.

He could hardly wait to tell his friends. Maybe now they'd shut up about his being gay. Except . . . what if Roxy found out he was blabbing about what they'd done?

On the other hand, it had sounded like she talked with her cellphone friend about what they did with boys. Besides, how could Carlos *not* tell his friends about tonight? He could barely stop himself from going to the window and shouting to the entire world: *Roxy Rodriguez and I made out!*

Forty-One

Next morning, Carlos's ma stared coldly at him, only thawing to say, "We'll talk this evening."

Raúl usually headed to his job at dawn, but today he waited for Carlos to prepare his backpack and told him, "I'll give you a ride to school."

Carlos sensed all this had to do with the events of the previous night.

"So . . ." Raúl pulled the truck out of the driveway. "Did your dad ever talk to you about girls?"

"Yeah," Carlos mumbled, squirming to adjust his seat belt.

"That's good." Raúl forced a tight-lipped smile. "So . . . he talked to you about condoms? About being careful not to get a girl pregnant?"

Actually, even though his pa constantly asked Carlos about the girls, he'd never talked to him about *that* stuff. Perhaps someone should've talked to his pa about it; then maybe he wouldn't have gotten Lupita pregnant. Carlos had mostly learned stuff from his friends.

"I already know all that," he grumbled to Raúl.

"Well . . ." Raúl stopped for a red light. "I told your mom I'll pick you up some condoms. She thinks you're too young, but I told her you need to protect yourself. There are a lot of new diseases out there."

Carlos stared out the window at the road ahead.

"Was the girl last night a girlfriend?" Raúl asked.

Carlos shifted in the truck seat. Had last night made Roxy his girlfriend? "I'm not sure," he told Raúl.

"Well, just remember . . ." Raúl tapped Carlos's head. "Think with your big head, not your little head." He jutted his chin toward Carlos's crotch. Carlos glanced away, embarrassed.

All during morning classes, he could barely concentrate. His mind swirled with images of boobs, worries about his ma, and his muddle about Roxy. He looked for her between classes, but didn't find her, and when he got to the lunchroom, she already sat chatting with her friends. Was she telling them about *him*?

He took his usual lunch seat, hoping she'd glance over. But she seemed almost to be ignoring him. Was she mad at him?

"Hey, how come you weren't on the bus this morning?" Toro asked.

"Huh? Um, I got a ride."

Playboy followed Carlos's gaze to Roxy. "You still chasing that? Give it up. She's too fine for a *pendejo* like you."

"Oh, yeah?" Suddenly, Carlos *had* to tell his friends. "Well, guess what, *pendejo*? She had me over last night."

Pulga put down his French fry. "Are you serious?"

"To her house?" Toro set down his burger.

Carlos nodded proudly. "Her mom wasn't home."

The group eyed him skeptically. "How far did you get?" Playboy asked.

Carlos shook his head. "That's personal."

Playboy sneered. "I guess that means you got *nada*."

"False alarm!" Pulga picked up his French fry again.

Carlos gritted his teeth, straining not to say more. But his buds' smart-ass attitudes irritated him. Besides, it wouldn't hurt to offer them a little something. "We made out."

"You and Roxy?" Toro raised his Coke to toast him. "Way to go, dudeness."

"Wow." Pulga nodded, impressed. "First base."

Carlos gave a modest shrug, although inside he felt elated. Finally, he'd gotten a little recognition.

"What else?" Playboy prodded. "Did she let you feel her boobs?"

Carlos clenched his jaw, determined not to be a blabbermouth. But the attention felt too good. "Um, yeah."

"Holy shit!" Pulga exclaimed.

Even Playboy dropped his jaw. "How'd you get her to do that, man?"

"I don't know. She just asked me to."

"No wonder she's ignoring you." Playboy gave a smirk.

Carlos sat up. "What do you mean?"

"The hookup rules." Playboy leaned back with an air of haughtiness. "Instead of admitting you're a slut, you pretend it didn't happen."

"But it *did* happen."

"And if you want more," Pulga said calmly, "you'll pretend it *didn't* happen."

Carlos didn't get it. "But what if we're dating?"

"Dude!" Playboy sighed patiently. "She had you over when her mom wasn't home. That's not a date. That's a hookup."

"Besides . . ." Pulga nodded. "You want to date a girl who hooks up?"

The question stumped Carlos. His secret fantasies were never this complicated.

"At least wait till after you've had sex with her before you decide if you want to date her," Playboy advised.

Carlos shook his head, his thoughts a jumble. How could his friends be so detached about all this? He turned to Toro, who'd become surprisingly silent, as though he didn't get it either. But hadn't he had sex with a girl once?

Compounding Carlos's woes, after lunch he saw that the GSA posters from the day before had been torn down or defaced. One now read:

                    NOT
        GAY IS ^ OKAY!
        DON'T
        ^ COME OUT FOR THE GSA

While another read:

                    SEXUALS
        TIRED OF HOMO~~PHOBIA~~?
                    THEM
        HELP US FIGHT ~~IT~~

Carlos didn't know whether to take the signs down or leave them.
For the rest of the school day, he struggled to sort out his mixed-up
thoughts about the last twenty-four hours. And it wasn't over yet. He
still had to face his ma.

Forty-Two

EVEN THOUGH ROXY had practically dissed Carlos at school, as soon as he got home, he raced to see if she was online. Upon spotting her name active on his buddy list, his fingers scurried across the keyboard. *Hey,* he IM-ed her. *Sup?*

He held his breath, awaiting her response. As each second passed, he felt more frantic. What if she kept pretending nothing had happened between them—*forever?*

To his relief, an IM from her popped up: *Nothin. Sup with u?*

Carlos's breath exploded from his lungs. He wanted to tell her *everything* that was up with him: about how pissed his ma had been last night; about how grown-up he'd felt to admit he'd been with a girl; about how Raúl had asked if she was his girlfriend; about how confused he felt by her ignoring him at school; about how his buds had tried to convince him his time with her had been just a hookup . . . And yet, he was unable to say any of that. He didn't want to sound like a mixed-up kid. And what if she told him his friends were right: It had been only a hookup?

Nothing much up here, he typed. *Gotta do homework.*

He hit send and slouched down in his chair, feeling like a total wuss.

Yeah, me too, Roxy replied. *Homework sucks. L8terz.*

Laterz, Carlos typed back, and stared at the computer,

wondering: Was he the only one in the world who felt all the sorts of stuff going on inside him?

He picked up the phone and dialed Sal. "Hey, why'd you call me last night?"

"Because *you* phoned *me*. My caller ID showed your call, so I phoned you back."

Carlos now remembered his attempted call. Feeling foolish, he slumped farther off his chair and onto the floor.

"Your mom sounded really pissed," Sal continued. "Where were you? What happened?"

Carlos laid down on the carpet, phone pressed to his ear, and told Sal about Roxy inviting him over, about making out, and about her showing him her—

"TMI!" Sal interrupted.

Carlos grinned at the irony. The one person whom he felt comfortable telling everything to was a gay guy who complained it was too much information.

"I can't believe how fast it all happened." Carlos stared at the framed praying mantis on the wall. "And at school she kind of ignored me. Why'd she do that?"

"I don't know. Maybe it was fast for her, too."

Carlos pondered that but didn't get it. If it was too fast for Roxy, why had she done it? "My friends say those are the rules."

"The rules for what?" Sal asked.

"For hooking up."

"So, was Roxy a hookup?"

"I don't know." Carlos was starting to feel mixed-up again. "What if that's all she wants?"

"Well, you've got to decide what *you* want. Have you told her you like her?"

"No." Carlos ran his fingers back and forth across the carpet weave, a little exasperated. "What if she doesn't like me?"

"Then you move on."

Carlos tugged at the carpet strands. "Maybe she's afraid people will think she's a hookup slut."

"Or maybe she is," Sal suggested.

Carlos sat up. "Hey, I don't like you talking about her like that."

"Oh, sorry." Sal's voice hinted sarcasm. "I forgot she's your girlfriend—except she's ignoring you."

Carlos gripped the phone tighter. "She's not my girlfriend yet."

"Right." Sal sighed. "I mean your hookup buddy—or what, exactly, is she?"

"Just drop it!" Carlos snapped. It seemed clear that Sal didn't like Roxy. He'd *never* liked her. So why had he continued to help Carlos even after Carlos couldn't pay him anymore?

"Dude . . ." Sal exhaled a long breath. "I'm sorry. I just don't want to see you get hurt."

"I'm not going to get hurt," Carlos mumbled.

Sal remained quiet and Carlos stood up. "Can you come over again Saturday?"

"Sorry, not this week. Javi and I are ushering at his cousin's wedding. Anyway, I think your makeover is done."

Carlos didn't feel done. He felt like he was still just starting. Why didn't the *Queer Eye* show cover this part: What happened *after* the makeover?

"Can we change topics?" Sal asked. "We set a date for the GSA meeting: next Wednesday after school. Okay?"

"Yeah, fine," Carlos grumbled, not really giving much thought to it. "Talk to you later."

He hung up and tried doing some homework, but his thoughts stayed too jumbled—not just because Sal had practically called Roxy a slut, but because he hadn't helped Carlos figure out what to do, other than to tell Roxy he liked her.

As if it was that simple, Carlos thought. His mood didn't improve much when his ma got home. She continued giving him the silent treatment, until they sat down to dinner.

"Did Raúl talk with you?" she asked, slicing her steak.

"Yeah."

"Do you have any questions about what he said?"

"No."

His ma stared across the table at him, her mean look softening a little. "Carlitos, I don't want this to happen again. Understand?" Her tone became stern once more. "You still have the same curfew: school nights, home by eleven, weekends by twelve."

Carlos stared at his steak and potatoes, losing his appetite. "No one else has to be home that early. Playboy doesn't even *have* a curfew."

"You're not Playboy." His ma laid down her fork. "You're living in my house and you abide by my rules. If you go to a girl's, I want to know about it."

"You're being ridiculous," Carlos muttered.

"I don't care," his ma replied. "I don't want any problems. And I don't want you lying to me again. For the next two weeks you're grounded."

Carlos slammed back in his chair. He was furious at his ma, even though he felt wrong for having lied.

After dinner he went online and told his friends about being grounded. They all agreed it sucked big-time, which made Carlos feel better. Then he went to Hot-or-Snot to give Roxy her daily "10." To his surprise, her rank had slipped a little.

Meanwhile, Playboy had taken down his profile altogether, now that he'd found BadAssGirl.

Carlos checked his own profile and saw his own rank slipping: down to an eight-point-three. He decided he'd better remove his profile too, before he joined Playboy as snot.

Forty-Three

ON THE BUS the following morning, Carlos and the guys listened to Playboy gripe about his hookup with BadAssGirl: "She turned out to be a poser. Although she'd made it sound like she was into no-strings sex, afterward she got all clingy, asking if I had a girlfriend and not wanting to let me go. She really did turn into my worst nightmare."

"Maybe she likes you," Toro suggested.

Carlos felt sorry for the girl. It seemed obvious she liked Playboy.

"That's her problem." Playboy gazed out the window. "I never told her I liked her."

Between classes at school, Carlos hoped to glimpse Roxy, though he no longer knew whether to wave hello or ignore her. It felt so weird to pretend as if nothing had happened between them. He now understood why Playboy only went out with girls from other schools.

Later that day at lunch, Pulga made his own announcement: "Carlotta just told me that since I won't date her, she's going to find someone else. No more after-school specials."

"She dumped you?" Toro asked.

Pulga frowned. "She didn't dump me. I'm the one who said I didn't want to date."

"Yeah," Playboy argued, "but *she's* the one who cut you off. Dude, you are *so* dumped."

Carlos wished he could offer Pulga some advice. But he was clueless enough with his own non-dating situation. So, he simply told Playboy, "Lay off him, man."

Forty-Four

SATURDAY MORNING, CARLOS woke up early, even though Sal wasn't coming over. As he cleansed, toned, and moisturized his face, he thought how much better he liked how he looked. Even his nose and ears no longer seemed freakishly huge. And when he ran some wax through his hair, he couldn't imagine how he had put up with his unruly mop.

After preparing a yogurt-and-granola breakfast, he cleaned up his room. And despite his annoying last phone conversation with Sal, Carlos nonetheless missed him.

He imagined Sal and Javier wearing tuxedoes at the wedding, and was glad they'd found each other. They seemed really good and happy together. Why couldn't Sal wish the same for Roxy and him?

In the afternoon, Carlos did the laundry—both his ma's and his. He had a lot more time to do things on weekends since no longer going to his pa's. But sometimes he missed his pa—a lot. And he even missed Lupita and Henry a little. But he didn't like to think about it too much. His life was confusing enough already.

He was surfing the web when Raúl tapped on the doorway.

"Here's a present for you." He tossed Carlos a small paper bag.

The color rose into Carlos's cheeks as he peered inside—at a box of condoms.

"This doesn't mean I'm telling you to have sex," Raúl clarified. "You should wait till you're married."

Carlos rolled his eyes. Wasn't that a bit hypocritical for a guy boning his ma to say?

"Or at least older," Raúl continued. "But I know how a guy thinks. So if you do have sex, protect yourself."

Whatever, Carlos thought, tossing the bag of condoms aside. But secretly, he felt a little excited. Might he actually get a chance to use them?

That evening, since he was grounded, he invited his friends over. They played computer games, listened to music, and tried to help Toro come up with a science project topic.

"Heh-heh-heh," Pulga chuckled. "Why don't you write about the deadly gases surrounding Uranus?"

"Or I'll help you explain how to make a hormone." Playboy smacked Toro on the shoulder. "Get it?"

Toro shook his head. "You guys are worthless."

Playboy leaned into the mirror scrutinizing a zit, and glanced at Carlos. "Hey, how did you get your skin to clear up?"

"First of all, by not eating crap." The comment was in retaliation for Playboy's complaint earlier in the evening that Carlos didn't have any chips or pretzels for the guys, only granola bars and fruit.

"What kind of pansy-ass shit is that?" Playboy had protested.

Carlos now proceeded to explain his twice daily regimen of cleanser, toner, and moisturizer. "And you need to drink eight to ten glasses of water a day—not soda or coffee, but *water*—to keep your skin hydrated."

"Who taught you all that?" Playboy smirked. "Your girly-boy?"

Carlos ignored him. "Also, I do a mud face mask once a week."

"You put mud on your face?" Playboy scrunched his nose. "You'd better stop jacking off. It's starting to rot your brain."

"It's not *real* mud." Carlos showed them the jar. "It's fun and it feels great. Watch . . ."

While his buds observed, Carlos unscrewed the cap, scooped out a dab of paste, and spread it on his face.

Playboy poked his finger in the jar and smeared some on Pulga's nose.

"Cut it out!" Pulga socked him.

"It smells like mint," Toro said, sniffing the jar. "Can I try it?"

"Yeah, me too!" Pulga said. A moment later, he and Toro were laughing like frolicking monkeys as they coated their faces. But Playboy wanted nothing to do with it.

The following evening, at a little past seven, Carlos's IM bell chimed. He glanced at his computer and his heart skipped a beat.

The message was from Roxy: *Sup? What r u doing?*

Carlos's fingers raced to the keyboard. *Nothin. How bout u?*

Bored, Roxy replied. *My mom went out with my lil bro. Wanna come over?*

As Carlos read Roxy's words, the image of her boobs virtually smashed through the computer screen. Trying to calm down, he typed: *I'm kinda grounded. Can't go out tonight.*

Roxy answered: ☹ *U been a bad boy?*

Yeah.

R u absolutely positively sure u can't sneak out? I'm reeeally bored. Pleeease?

Carlos wiped the sweat from his own real-life sad face, wondering if he couldn't somehow sneak out. But his ma would surely kill him.

If I could I would, he wrote, *but I really can't.*

Roxy replied: ☹ ☹ ☹ ☹ ☹ ☹ ☹

Carlos's heart wrenched in anguish—as did his loins. The keys clacked beneath his fingers. *Me ☹ too.*

That night, he climbed into bed early, unable to contain his imaginings of Roxy—and all the stuff they could've done together if he'd gone to her place. It no longer mattered to him if they were a couple or just a hookup. She wanted him. And more than ever, he wanted her.

Forty-Five

DURING THE NEXT days, Carlos spent hours zombielike, thinking only of Roxy.

On Wednesday at the condiment counter, when she turned to him and whispered, "Cheerleading practice was canceled. You want to come over after school?" he immediately gulped, "Sure!"

"Great." She gave an impish grin and glanced at his table. "But don't tell your little pals, okay? I don't want the whole school blabbing about us."

Carlos nodded obediently. As Roxy strutted to her table, Carlos ambled to his own, determined to keep his mouth shut. But Playboy immediately confronted him.

"You two just booked a hookup, didn't you?"

"Shut up!" Carlos plopped his tray down. "I'm not supposed to say anything." But he couldn't help adding: "It's for after school."

"I thought you were grounded," Toro reminded him.

"Oh, shit!" In his euphoria, Carlos had forgotten about that.

Pulga gave him a wily grin. "But if it's for after school, how will mommy know?"

Carlos broke into an uncontrollable smile and gazed across the lunchroom at Roxy, imagining her T-shirt lifting for him once more.

Minutes later, his fantasy was shattered.

"Hey!" Sal called to Carlos outside the cafeteria. "Don't forget our meeting after school!"

"Huh? What meeting?"

"The GSA!" Sal frowned. "Don't tell me you forgot. Harris is coming to close us down if anyone even whispers the word 'sex.' Espie is
out sick. You might be the only straight guy, so we really need you."

"Um, okay." Carlos nodded. As he watched Sal disappear into the
hallway crowd, he felt his heart sink. How could he have forgotten
the GSA? He couldn't bag out on Sal. Yet, how could he bail on Roxy?
Who knew how far she might let him get this time?

During Geometry, the teacher led the class through one small
angle formula after another, while Carlos struggled to solve his own
problem.

If Sal were straight, Carlos could simply tell him the truth. A straight
guy would understand. But Sal wasn't straight or exactly fond of
Roxy—certainly not enough to excuse Carlos from the GSA meeting.

By the end of last period, Carlos had failed to solve the dilemma.
But he knew he couldn't pass up Roxy. When the final bell rang, he
slinked out to his bus, feeling like a total slimeball for blowing off the
GSA. And yet, once he arrived home, he could barely control his
excitement. He tossed his backpack onto his bed, grabbed the pack of
condoms, and raced out the door toward Roxy's.

Forty-Six

ROXY ANSWERED THE door biting into a shiny red apple. A cropped T-shirt revealed her midriff. "Want some?"

Carlos pulled his gaze up to her face. "Huh?"

She laughed, tossing him the apple. He barely caught it as Roxy led him into the living room. "Come on! My fave soap is on."

Carlos took his same sofa seat as before, next to Roxy. Not really sure what to do with the apple, he took a bite from the spot she'd already bitten into and handed it back. "Thanks."

On the TV, a soap opera doctor discussed with a patient a highly delicate operation. One accidental slip, and the woman could end up brain-dead.

Apparently moved by the scene, Roxy tossed her apple aside and intertwined her fingers with Carlos's. Instantly all of Carlos's guilt about choosing Roxy over Sal's GSA meeting subsided.

Carlos grew warm beneath his jean jacket as he debated his next move. Since Roxy had let him kiss her before, should he feel free to simply lean over and kiss her again? Or should he keep asking permission all the time? As soon as the program switched to a commercial, he turned to face her. To his relief, she took the cue.

Within seconds, his lips, the sweetness of apples, and the faint, salty taste of skin all mixed together.

"Hey, take it easy!" Roxy ordered with a giggle.

"Um, sorry." Carlos drew back.

"Relax," Roxy whispered and pulled his face to her chest.

His ear pressed against her boob. "I can feel your heart beating," he whispered. "I never heard anyone's heartbeat before."

"Uh-huh," Roxy replied, pressing his nose deeper into her cleavage.

As Carlos listened to her heart, feeling so close, he wanted to know everything about her: what she ate for breakfast; why her parents had split up; if she missed her dad; why she didn't have a boyfriend . . .

Carlos pulled his face from between her boobs. "Can I ask you something?"

"Wait till the next commercial." Roxy whispered and pushed his face back into her cleavage. "Can you do like you did last time?"

Eager to please, Carlos lifted her T-shirt. The scent of cherry perfume wafted up his nose and into his brain. As he kissed her chest, her breath came harder and faster.

When he raised his head to gulp a mouthful of air, she clutched his hair and begged, "Keep going! Please, don't stop!"

"Um . . ." He cleared his throat. "I think I'm about to burst."

Her magical green eyes widened. "Don't!" She abruptly pushed him off her and he feared she was angry, except that she was grinning.

He nearly fell off the couch when she whispered, "Pull down your pants!"

Forty-Seven

CARLOS GAZED UP at Roxy, certain he'd heard wrong. Had she truly told him to pull his pants down? To be sure, he asked, "For real?"

"Yes!" She tugged at his belt, giggling. "Hurry up!"

A million thoughts collided in Carlos's brain. How was this happening? Were girls actually as horny as in his fantasies? What if her mom came home? But the urgency in his pants overrode the concerns in his brain.

Hands quivering, Carlos fumbled to unclasp his SEXY belt buckle. Why wouldn't the damn thing open? Fortunately, Roxy's fingers worked more nimbly. Carlos raised his hips and tugged his jeans down to his knees.

"Your underwear, too." Roxy sighed impatiently. "Hurry!"

Carlos hesitated. He'd never let anybody see him in such a state of excitement. What if Roxy thought his thing was too small? What if she laughed at it?

Don't look, okay? he wanted to tell her. But he didn't want to sound like a kid. Instead, he closed his own eyes.

As he tugged his briefs down, Roxy giggled, but not as though she were laughing at it—more as if she liked it. "Mmm . . ."

Emboldened, Carlos cracked one eye open. Roxy hovered above his lap, grinning as if she'd just unwrapped a present. Carlos slammed his eye shut again, both embarrassed and thrilled.

Roxy's warm fingertips touched Carlos and a little zap of electricity surged through him. He wondered if she had felt it too, since she abruptly pulled away.

Then she gasped as the front door rattled. "Shit! It's my mom!"

Forty-Eight

CARLOS LEAPED OFF the couch, yanking his pants nearly up to his neck. His heart beat wildly as he struggled with his buckle, barely clasping it before the front door swung open.

"Hi, Mom!" Roxy waved casually at an older but still good-looking version of herself: the same highlighted hair, hip-tight skirt, and killer breasts. In each hand the woman carried a plastic grocery bag. Beside her stood a small boy—Roxy's little brother, no doubt.

"We were just watching TV." Roxy smiled innocently. "This is Carlos."

Carlos guiltily buried his hands deep in his pockets. "Um, hi."

Mrs. Rodriguez's eyes flashed between Carlos and Roxy, obviously not believing her daughter. "Didn't I tell you last time you're not allowed to have boys over when I'm not here?"

What does she mean by "last time"? Carlos wondered. How many other guys had Roxy invited over? Did she get into their pants too?

"Mom!" Roxy averted her eyes from Carlos. "You're embarrassing me!"

"No," her mom retorted. *"You're* embarrassing *me*! What are the neighbors going to think?"

"I don't care what they think!" Roxy flung her hair back over her shoulder.

Roxy's mom wagged a finger at Carlos. "I don't want you here when I'm not home. Understand?"

"Mom!" Roxy repeated. "Stop it! I'm not a child."

"Then stop acting like one!" her mom yelled back.

Carlos ducked as if dodging bullets while Roxy's little brother aimed the remote control toward the TV, changing the channel to cartoons.

"I hate you!" Roxy screamed at her mom. Her body shook with rage, though she looked about to cry. "I hate you!" she reiterated, storming out of the room and into the hall. A moment later, a door slammed.

"Um, nice meeting you," Carlos said politely, like Sal had taught him. Then he hustled past Roxy's mom as fast as his legs could carry him.

It hadn't been how he'd imagined meeting the mom of the girl he adored. In fact, he couldn't recall any mother or ticked-off daughter ever appearing in his dreams. It had scared him to see Roxy so wild with anger.

He shuffled along the sidewalk, trying to calm himself. The whole afternoon seemed like a bummer. He'd come so close to getting laid—or at least getting oral. But he hadn't even gotten that.

Yet at least he'd made a little progress. Despite his shyness—or perhaps because of it—he'd felt an undeniable thrill at letting Roxy see and touch him. That was worth something. With that thought, he felt better, and crossed the street toward his apartment complex.

But as he got to his building, his heart sank even deeper. A lone figure, stiff and still, waited on the top step of the staircase. His gaze bore down on Carlos. And Carlos suddenly remembered that his time with Roxy had come at a cost.

Forty-Nine

FROM THE TOP step of the tile staircase, Sal gazed silently down at Carlos. His eyes said a million things in a single hurt and angry beam directed straight at Carlos.

"Why didn't you come to the GSA meeting?"

"Um . . ." Carlos grabbed the handrail as his mind fumbled for an excuse. Once again, he wished Sal were straight. Then Carlos would simply explain that he'd passed up a boring school meeting for the prospect of getting laid. In his straight-teen-guy world, that possibility trumped any other commitment, especially with another guy.

But Sal definitely wasn't straight, and Carlos couldn't conjure up any convincing excuse for having missed the GSA. He lamely uttered, "I forgot."

"You *forgot*?" Sal bolted up from the stair step, his eyes on fire. "How the hell could you forget? I reminded you at lunch."

"I know." Carlos grappled for words. "I mean, I forgot I had something else to do."

"Like *what*? What else was so important?"

"Um . . ." Carlos dug into his pocket for his keys while trying to come up with a believable lie. "I had a dentist's appointment. I . . . I'd forgotten about it."

Sal gave him a piercing look. "You'd better not be lying."

"I'm not." Carlos's voice sounded shrilly false even to himself. He hated lying to Sal, but there would be other GSA meetings he could attend. What was the big deal? He hurried up the steps and opened the apartment door. "Um, you want to come in?"

He watched Sal's face soften slightly. Apparently, he'd bought Carlos's lie.

"Thanks." Sal stepped inside. "So how was the dentist?"

"Okay." Carlos swallowed the guilty knot in his throat and led Sal toward the kitchen, quickly changing topics. "You want something to eat?"

He pulled from the fridge some pears his ma had bought and handed one to Sal. Although the fruit was barely ripe, the time with Roxy had made Carlos too hungry to care. He took a crisp bite and noticed Sal eyeing him curiously.

"No cavities?" Sal asked. "Your mouth isn't sore or numb or anything?"

"No, I'm fine. So, um, how was the meeting?"

Sal's lips angled into a frown. "There was no meeting."

"Huh?" Carlos stopped chewing his pear. "What do you—?"

"No one showed up," Sal interrupted. "I told you, Espie was sick. Carlotta had to take a math make-up exam. And Vicky couldn't get out of band rehearsal. No new students came. Our posters were no help. The meeting consisted of Mr. Quiñones, Harris, and me staring at each other."

As Carlos listened, he could barely swallow the chunk of pear in his throat. He truly felt sorry for Sal, imagining him in the silent library, with no other students to back him up and Hard-Ass Harris scowling at him.

The image made Carlos feel even guiltier, both for ditching the meeting and for lying about it. "Well, I promise I'll be there next time."

"Forget it." Sal shook his head despondently. "There isn't going to be a next time. No one cares about a GSA."

"I do," Carlos said, trying to cheer Sal up and also make himself feel better. "I care about it."

Sal gave him a skeptical smirk. "I'm not going through this again. It's not worth it."

"Yes, it is," Carlos insisted, though he felt a little nuts doing so. Why didn't he just let the thing die? He'd never wanted to participate in the group in the first place. But seeing his friend so dejected had made Carlos's guilt grow deeper.

"You were right," Carlos pressed on, "Every day I hear all the name-calling, and it's not even toward gay people. It's like you said, 'Homophobia hurts everybody.' We need the GSA. Remember the Gandhi quote: 'Be the change you wish to see in the world'? I'll be there next time, no matter what. I promise."

Sal peered at him a little cockeyed. Carlos couldn't blame him. Where was all this stuff spewing out of his mouth coming from? If Carlos really believed it, then why had he crapped out on the meeting?

For the first time that afternoon, a smile slowly creased its way across Sal's face. "You really promise?"

"Absolutely!" Carlos beamed, his guilt finally subsiding. As he took another bite from his pear, he heard the front door open.

"Hi, guys!" His ma paused in the kitchen doorway to kick her shoes off, smiling. She'd gotten over her anger at Carlos, even though he was still grounded. "How did it go today? Oh, before I forget," she told Carlos. "I finally made you a dentist appointment."

With her words, Carlos ceased chewing his pear. His entire world seemed to stop, even his breathing. As Sal's smile evaporated, his eyes flooded with hurt.

"Sal?" Carlos's ma asked. "Would you like to join us for dinner?"

Sal remained silent, his eyes trained on Carlos as the hurt in them transformed into fury.

"No thanks." He pitched his pear aside, rushing out the door. "See you later, Mrs. Amoroso."

"Sal, wait!" Carlos chased after him, but Sal was already bounding down the building staircase. At the bottom landing, Carlos caught up, grabbing hold of his arm. "Wait!"

Sal whirled around, shaking him off. "You goddamn liar! What the hell was that shit about being the change in the world?"

Carlos opened his mouth in defense but something in his throat grew larger, making his voice not quite itself. "Roxy invited me over. I almost got *laid*!"

"So?" Sal's eyes were indifferent. "Like that makes everything okay? We had a deal, remember? Obviously your makeover barely scratched the surface—'cause who you are inside is a lot crappier than you ever looked outside!"

Carlos winced as if a giant fist had slammed into his stomach. Sal spun around and stomped away, while Carlos watched silently, trying to regain his bearings.

Couldn't Sal understand how important having a girlfriend and getting laid were to Carlos? It would mean he'd stop being a kid. And yet, as Carlos shuffled back up the stairway, he couldn't help agreeing with Sal: Inside, he felt like crap.

Fifty

CARLOS SHUFFLED BACK into the kitchen, where his ma was rinsing lettuce.

"Is everything okay between you and Sal?"

Carlos stared down at the tile floor. What could he say? That he'd bagged out on Sal in hopes of getting laid before she got home?

"Everything's fine," he mumbled.

He withdrew to his bedroom and flopped onto his bed. Staring at the made-over walls, he tried to sort out the events of the afternoon.

He wished he could go back to lunchtime that day and start over. But would he really choose any differently? How could he have turned down Roxy?

Even though he felt like crap about flaking out on Sal, wouldn't he have felt worse if he'd passed up Roxy's invitation?

Carlos brought his hand up to scratch his nose and smelled the lingering aroma of Roxy's cherry-scented perfume. In his memory, he could still feel her tender fingertips where no other person had ever touched him. Hadn't that been worth everything?

Besides, he hadn't been the only one to bag out on Sal: Espie, Vicky, and Carlotta had flaked out too. What if Carlos had turned down Roxy and shown up for the GSA, with only Sal, Mr. Quiñones, and Hard-Ass Harris there? What kind of pathetic meeting would that have been?

Maybe Sal was right. Maybe they should forget about the GSA idea.

All evening long, Carlos's thoughts bounced back and forth

between Sal and Roxy. After dinner, he went to his computer, hoping to find her online. But she wasn't. Carlos's buds IM-ed, asking how far he'd gotten with her, but Carlos didn't feel like going into it.

I'll tell u tomorrow, he replied.

To which Playboy messaged back: *Didn't get any, huh?*

Annoyed, Carlos went offline. He tried doing some homework while listening to music. But to complete his crappy day, his headphones broke.

When his ma came to say good night, he told her about them. "Can I have money for some new ones?"

"Sorry, *mi amor* . . ." She kissed him on the forehead. "But things are tight right now."

Carlos turned away, even more depressed.

Near midnight, he climbed into bed and easily summoned a fantasy of Roxy. But afterward, he felt even guiltier than ever before.

Fifty-One

THE FOLLOWING MORNING, as Carlos bounced down the bus aisle, Vicky asked, "How was the GSA meeting?"

Carlos felt the color creep up his cheeks. Ever since waking, he'd been fretting about how Sal might react to him at school, but he hadn't foreseen Vicky confronting him. "Um, I didn't go."

"You *didn't go?*" Today she was wearing Goth black, and her brow furrowed beneath her ghoul-white face powder. "Sal was counting on you!"

"I know." Carlos gripped the seat handle to steady himself.

"Why are you in the GSA, anyway?" Vicky turned away. "I knew you were a poser."

"No, I'm not!" Carlos argued, though he wondered: *Am I posing? As what?*

He swayed down the bus aisle toward the back row, where his friends crowded around him.

"So, what happened with Roxy?"

"Tell us!"

"Spill the dirt, man."

"Promise you won't tell anyone?" Carlos said, and in a low voice he started to relate his Roxy progress.

"She got into your pants?" Toro whispered excitedly.

"Not bad!" Playboy patted Carlos on the back. "At least you got some oral."

"Um, not exactly," Carlos confessed. "Her ma came home."

"Holy shit!" Pulga exclaimed. "What did she do?"

"Mostly yelled at Roxy. She told me not to go over there if she wasn't home."

"Parents suck," Playboy proclaimed.

"Yeah," the rest of them agreed.

During the remainder of the ride, Carlos's thoughts focused on Roxy. How would she act toward him now that she'd dived into his pants? Surely she'd have to acknowledge him at least a teensy bit more.

At lunchtime, he gazed expectantly across the cafeteria. Roxy chatted and laughed with her friends, but she barely gave Carlos a crumb of a smile. He didn't get it. How could she be that way? Even though his buds claimed those were the rules, it was starting to annoy him. He wanted to talk to her about it, but what could he say?

Um, Roxy, how come you want to get me naked but won't talk to me at school?

His mood didn't perk up any after lunch, when he waved to Sal in the hall. "'S'up?"

He figured Sal would yell or glare at him, but at least he'd be on his way to getting over yesterday's blowout.

Instead, Sal walked right by, as though Carlos didn't even exist.

Carlos's smile sagged. Once again, he wished Sal were straight. A straight Sal would've had thicker skin and not gotten so upset and hurt about the whole thing. After their fight, Straight Sal would've gone to bed that night (without cleaning, toning, and moisturizing) and gotten over it the next day, when Carlos walked up to him in the hall and socked him in the arm.

"Cut it out!" Sal would've punched him back. "*Pendejo* homo!"

And things would've returned to normal, simple as that. After school, Straight Sal would go to Carlos's and they'd eat about a million bags of greasy potato chips and sugar cookies, along with several cans of *non*-diet root beer, and afterward have a burping competition.

Then they'd lie on the carpet listening to Los Lonely Boys and not talk—they wouldn't have to. They'd just know they were bound by friendship, no matter what.

And when things got too quiet, Straight Sal would ask Carlos, "So how far did you get with Roxy?"

If only, Carlos thought, and watched Sal disappear down the hallway.

Fifty-Two

IN THE FOLLOWING days, Carlos tried to put his quarrel with Sal out of his mind—mostly by playing an endless loop of his matinee with Roxy. He left out the part where her mom had walked in.

Her warning to Carlos not to come around when she wasn't home meant Roxy and he would have to find other ways to be together. Maybe they could go to a movie, like other couples. Except, he'd never invited a girl to anything.

And yet, despite what Sal had said during their fight, Carlos felt his makeover *had* changed him inside, making him feel a teeny bit braver. But, bold enough to ask Roxy out?

That weekend, Carlos finally got off restriction. Saturday afternoon, he saw Roxy was online. Sweat blistered on his forehead as he typed: *Sup? U wanna go see a movie tonight?*

He hit send and waited, leg jiggling impatiently at the computer, not certain what he'd do if she told him no . . . or what he'd do if she actually said *yes*.

When the IM chime finally sounded, he jumped.

Can't, she replied. *Going to a concert with friends. Sorry.*

Carlos studied the message. What concert? What friends? Why didn't she invite him to go too?

But she'd probably gotten tickets long ago, he rationalized, before she and he were on getting-naked terms. And now the concert was no doubt sold-out. Plus, she was most likely going with her girl friends.

Well, he wrote, *u wanna go to the movies tomorrow?*

Once again, he stared at the computer screen for what seemed like hours.

At last, her reply came: *Look, not a good idea. Let's just hook up again sometime, ok?*

Carlos analyzed the IM even longer than he had the last one, trying to make sense of it. What did she mean by "not a good idea" and "just hook up?" He paced the room, pausing every once in a while to reread the message, trying to decode its meaning.

That evening, he invited his buds over after dinner. When Playboy and Pulga arrived, he showed them Roxy's IM.

"Obviously, she just wants to be friends with benefits," Pulga suggested. "She doesn't want to date."

But, to Carlos, that didn't make sense. "If she wants to get into my pants, why not date me?"

"She probably doesn't want the hassles," Playboy explained. "The drama and pain."

Pulga laid a consoling hand on Carlos's shoulder. "Dating causes pain."

Carlos shook his head. Wasn't *not* dating Roxy and only hooking up also causing him pain?

"You know how many guys would give up a week of jacking off to get Roxy in their pants?" Pulga's voice rang with admiration. "Don't screw it up, *pendejo*. Look at how Carlotta screwed things up by wanting to date. Remember the *numero uno* rule of hookups: Don't get attached. It's suicide."

"Just lean back and enjoy." Playboy punched Carlos. "Forget the hassles of dating. Stop being so needy."

Toro arrived after that, bringing over a new video game. Carlos wished Toro had been there for the conversation so he could've gotten his point of view. But the guys wanted to play the new game and Carlos didn't feel like rehashing the subject.

Later, after his buds left, Carlos stared at Roxy's J-peg a long while, thinking about everything Playboy and Pulga had said. Was he being needy? Maybe he should be happy with what he was getting. And yet, he also remembered Sal's comment after the first hookup with Roxy: "You've got to decide what *you* want."

Carlos got ready for bed and curled beneath the covers, eager to summon forth one of his favorite Roxy fantasies. But instead, the image of her at some concert, laughing and having fun with her friends, kept intruding. And the picture didn't include him.

In spite of what Pulga had said, Carlos wondered: Was he even getting a "friend with benefits," or only the benefits?

Fifty-Three

CARLOS'S DOUBTS ABOUT Roxy only deepened the following week. At lunch, some senior dude stopped by her table. He was a little taller than Carlos and definitely better built, with a cocky swagger and confident smile. As the dude talked with her, Roxy grinned back, starry-eyed and laughing.

Carlos shifted in his metal chair. Who was the guy? Was he one of the boys Roxy's mom had implied when she said, "I told you last time . . ."? Or one of the "friends" Roxy had gone to the concert with? Why was she talking openly to him in front of everyone and yet treated Carlos like some embarrassing secret?

During afternoon classes, Carlos tried to flush away the image of Senior Dude and Roxy, but it kept bobbing back up his mind.

When Carlos arrived home, he marched directly to his computer. From his buddy list he could see Roxy was online. In spite of her mom's warning, he asked, *Can I come over?*

He watched the screen, hoping she'd say yes so that he could get a little reassurance. The clock on his monitor showed the passing minutes. Why wasn't she responding?

Finally, an IM chimed: *Not today . . . Sorry . . . L8terz.*

A sickening feeling seeped into Carlos's stomach. Why didn't Roxy want him to come over? She obviously wasn't at choreography class, cheerleading, or chorus. Was it because Senior Dude was coming over for a hookup?

Carlos peeled his jean jacket off, feeling warm, and threw it on the floor. Then he stretched his fingers and typed: *Y not?*

He hit send and waited, balling his fingers into fists, while crazy thoughts of Roxy doing it with Senior Dude on her couch whipped through his brain.

At last, an IM popped up: *U can't come over cuz I said u can't. I don't have to give u a reason. LATER!!!*

A wave of anger surged inside Carlos. He slammed the keyboard tray beneath his desk, muttering, "Bitch!"

Immediately, he flushed with embarrassment. He'd never called a girl that before—and he'd definitely never imagined saying it about the girl he cherished.

Fifty-Four

CARLOS STORMED AWAY from his computer and into the kitchen. From the cupboard, he yanked out a jumbo bag of potato chips dating from pre-Sal. Weeks had passed since he'd eaten any junk. Now, he devoured the entire bag of chips and guzzled a liter of Coke, while he tried to calm his frenzied thoughts. *Doesn't she like me anymore? Maybe she never liked me in the first place. But then why did she make out and nearly go down on me?*

Unable to come up with an answer, he scarfed down some old, crystallized ice cream he found at the back of the freezer.

When he'd stomped back to his computer, he found an IM from Pulga: *Sup, pendejo?*

Carlos wanted to tell him how furious and confused he felt about Roxy. But he didn't want to keep sounding needy. *Nothin,* he said instead. *Sup with u?*

Nothin, Pulga replied, *just sorta thinking about Carlotta . . . Can I tell u something? Promise u won't tell the other guys?*

Okay. Carlos sat forward in his chair. *I promise.*

After a long moment, Pulga replied, *The truth is . . . I really like Carlotta, even if she is freaky tall. When we're together, she makes me feel great. I even sort of like her being so tall. Weird, huh?*

Carlos stared at the message. Was this the same Pulga who had warned him that getting attached was suicide? Was he now joking? To check, Carlos asked, *For real?*

Yeah, Pulga messaged back. *I feel like such a loser . . . U think I'm a loser?*

It hurt to hear his friend put himself down, especially when he recalled how Carlotta had told him she liked Pulga.

Ur not a loser, Carlos typed. *U know she likes you, don't you?*

U really think so? Pulga replied.

Yeah! She told me so when we were making GSA posters. She wants 2 date u! What more do u want?

The computer screen was still, as if Pulga were considering what Carlos had said. Then came his response: *Playboy says I'd be pussy-whipped crawling back to her. I'd feel like a total loser.*

Who cares what Playboy says? Carlos argued. He remembered the advice Sal had once given him: *Just tell her that you like her. What have you got to lose? U already feel like a loser anyway.*

True, Pulga agreed. *U really think I should tell her?*

Yeah, Carlos encouraged him. *Just do it.*

After a few more messages, Pulga logged off.

To Carlos, the solution to Pulga's situation had seemed so simple. But his own crisis continued to baffle him.

Maybe he should've told Roxy that he liked her from the start, as Sal had said. Perhaps he should tell her that *now.* Except his situation was different from Pulga's. Roxy had never told Carlos she liked him. Was he willing to be the first to say it?

A shiver ran down his back. Compared to pulling his pants down, this felt way more risky.

Fifty-Five

THE NEXT DAY at lunch, Carlos stared across the lunchroom, his stomach grinding. Senior Dude was not only talking to Roxy, he was sitting at her table.

His buds followed his gaze. Toro asked, "Why is that guy sitting with her?"

"I don't know." Carlos stabbed the tomato on his burger. "And I don't care."

Playboy stretched his arms, patting Carlos on the back. "Well, you know what they say: If you love someone, let 'em go. If they don't come back, hunt 'em down and kill 'em."

Carlos pondered Playboy's suggestion, his head burning. For Roxy to ignore him had been annoying. For her to diss him with another guy was enraging. All afternoon, in every class, Carlos shifted in his chair, debating his options, till he finally made a choice.

When the final bell rang, he trekked slowly toward Roxy's homeroom, his heart galloping ahead of him. Amidst the clamor of students, Roxy stood at her locker with her friends, talking and giggling.

Carlos shoved his fists into his jean jacket, fighting the urge to back out. Steeling himself with all his courage, he called out to her, "'S'up?"

Roxy darted a glance at him, briefly nodded, and returned her attention to her friends.

As she turned away, Carlos felt his resolve collapse. Maybe this wasn't such a good idea. But he had to do it. He swallowed the lump in his throat and burst out, "Hey, can we talk a sec?"

The words boomed louder than he'd meant, echoing against the metal lockers.

Roxy's group turned instantly silent, peering at him.

"Please?" he quickly added.

Roxy said something to her friends. Then she stepped toward him, her beautiful lips pressed into an irritated line. "What's so important?"

"Um . . ." Carlos felt the sweat dampening his neck. "Can we go talk somewhere?"

Roxy gave him a hard-jawed look, as if considering. "Look, I've got to get to cheerleading practice. What is it?"

Carlos knew what he needed to say and he realized he'd better say it quickly, before he completely lost his nerve. His heart pounded in his chest. He looked straight into her eyes and said it: "I really like you."

Sweat drenched his collar as he waited for Roxy's response.

She took a deep breath and let it out. "Carlos . . ." Her face softened with concern. "It was just hooking up, okay?"

He felt a sting, as if a needle had pierced his heart. How could she say that, especially after he'd held her in his arms, tasted the salt on her skin, listened to her heart beating beneath her breast? He'd allowed her to see him practically naked, like no one else on earth had ever seen him. And by telling her he liked her, he felt as if he'd bared his soul to her too.

"Roxy!" her friends called.

"I've got to go," she told Carlos, and sauntered back to her friends.

"What did he want?" one asked.

"Nothing," Roxy replied. "Let's go." And with that, she strode away, not looking back.

Carlos braced himself against a locker, feeling his world crumbling around him. How could he have been so stupid? As he leaned against the cold metal, he finally got it: Only in his mind had the relationship with Roxy been more than physical.

His eyes went blurry with emotion as he hurriedly weaved through the crowded hallway and traipsed home.

When he arrived at his apartment, he threw himself onto the bed, wishing he'd never said anything to Roxy. Had he seriously imagined that by simply telling her he liked her she might respond in kind? He felt like an idiot for thinking Roxy might want to be his girlfriend. His makeover had been a total waste of time.

On the wall above the painted headboard loomed the dried-up praying mantis framed by Sal. This was all Sal's fault. He'd encouraged Carlos to believe he stood a chance with Roxy. And he'd planted in Carlos's brain the dumb idea of telling Roxy he liked her.

Carlos reached up and yanked down the mantis. He hurled the Plexiglas box across the room, where it thudded onto the carpet. Then Carlos lay down again and brought his knees to his chest, wanting to shrivel up and die.

Fifty-Six

CARLOS LAY CURLED in bed when the doorbell startled him. At the front door he found Toro.

"What happened to you?" Toro grinned at him. "You look like *caca*."

"Thanks," Carlos grumbled and led Toro to his room, where he plopped onto the bed again.

From the desk chair, Toro pitched aside a dirty T-shirt and sat down, surveying the once-again disheveled room. "Why didn't you ride the bus home?"

"Didn't feel like it."

Toro gave him a long look. "Is this about Roxy?"

Carlos sighed, his chest tight and hurting. "Can I ask you something? How did you do it? How did you keep from getting attached to Leticia?"

Toro glanced down at the carpet and cleared his throat. "I need to, um, come clean to you about something." He gazed up at Carlos, his eyes wavering. "This is really hard for me. Promise you won't tell the other guys?"

"Sure." Carlos leaned forward on the bed. He'd already sort of figured out what Toro was going to say: that he'd never really had sex with Leticia, that he'd made the whole thing up by downloading some chick's photo off the web. He wasn't prepared for what Toro actually said.

"I think, um . . ." Toro gave a nervous cough and shuffled his feet. "I think I'm gay."

Carlos stared, speechless, disbelieving his ears. Yet hadn't Sal and

Javier told him Toro was gay? Wasn't Toro always carrying muscle magazines, staring at pics of guys? Hadn't he gotten noticeable wood during that wrestling match freshman year?

Nevertheless, Toro *couldn't* be gay. He'd been Carlos's friend since second grade. They'd slept over at each other's houses, sharing the same bed sometimes. They'd draped their arms around each other's shoulders, drunk out of the same soda can . . . If Toro was gay, why hadn't he ever said anything?

"I've wanted to tell you," Toro now explained. "You're the one person who I figured would understand, since you're friends with Sal."

Carlos shook his head. This was all too much: Sal ditching him, Roxy crushing his heart, and now a lifelong best bud telling him he wasn't who Carlos had thought he'd been.

"You're not gay," Carlos announced.

Toro peered back at him with a curious look. "Well . . . I've tried not to be, but . . . I've never liked girls that way. There never was a Leticia. I figured since you're friends with Sal—"

"Would you shut up about that?" Carlos cut him off. "I can't deal with this right now, okay?"

Toro hung his head. Nearly whispering, he asked, "Do you want me to go?"

"Yeah," Carlos replied, his temples throbbing.

Toro stood and quietly shuffled out of the room, like a prisoner accepting his sentence.

And Carlos felt like a creep. Why was he being so hard on Toro? After all, he'd accepted Sal as gay. But that was different. Sal had been honest with Carlos; he'd never lied to him. And yet, who was Carlos to judge anyone for lying? Sal had been right about him: He did need an inner makeover—an *extreme* one.

He sprang from the bed and caught Toro as he was about to open the front door. "Wait!"

Toro turned, wiping his face, and Carlos saw that his eyes were wet.

"I'm sorry," Carlos told him. "It's just . . ." His voice trailed off. He was uncertain what to say. "Why didn't you tell me before?"

"Because I wasn't sure." Toro's voice rasped. "I didn't want people calling me names and talking trash about me. I'm still the same person."

Carlos gave a weary shrug. "Who cares what other people think?"

"Then you're okay with it?" Toro's eyes glimmered.

"I guess." Carlos scratched his neck, still absorbing the news. Now, along with everything else in his life, he'd have to get used to one of his best buds being gay. "I mean, yeah."

"You won't tell anyone?" Toro whispered. "What do you think the guys would say?"

"I don't know. I won't tell them. I've got enough to deal with. If you want to tell—"

"I'm not telling them!" Toro gave his head a vigorous shake. "The only reason I told you was because you're friends with . . ."

Carlos cut him a sharp look.

"Well," Toro resumed meekly, "you *are* friends with Sal, aren't you?"

"I don't know." Carlos sighed. "He won't talk to me 'cause I didn't show for the GSA meeting."

Toro raised his eyebrows in confusion. "But that was your deal with him, wasn't it?"

"Yeah." Carlos frowned. "And I screwed it up."

"Oh." Toro sounded let down. "I'd hoped maybe—you know—you could see if—I don't know—if you could get him to give me some advice."

Oh, great, Carlos thought, feeling even more like he'd screwed things up royally.

"*You* ask him," he told Toro.

Toro shook his head. "I'd feel too weird without you. When does the GSA meet again? I could go with you."

Carlos dropped onto the sofa, resting his head in his hands. "It's not going to meet again. Nobody showed up for it."

"No one?" Toro sounded even more downcast.

"It's not my fault!" Carlos crossed his arms.

Toro gave a shrug and rested his hand on the doorknob. "I'd better go." He paused as if thinking about something. Then he removed his palm from the knob and extended his hand toward Carlos, his entire face a question mark.

Carlos shook it immediately, saying, "*Pendejo.*"

For the first time that afternoon, Toro grinned—and so did Carlos.

Fifty-Seven

THAT NIGHT, CARLOS dreamed about boobs. Nothing unusual about that, except . . . something felt odd about this particular pair of dream breasts. Still dreaming, he walked to his dresser mirror. What he saw made him scream in horror. The breasts belonged to him: He'd turned into a girl.

He woke in a sweat, slamming his hand onto the alarm clock.

"Carlos, wake up!" his ma called from the hall. "You'll be late for school."

He caught his breath. The last thing he wanted was to go to school—and see Roxy.

He dragged himself out of bed and peered into the mirror, cringing. Although he hadn't grown boobs, he looked like crap. His highlights were growing out, making his hair look dorkily streaky, and his face was breaking out again.

He thought back to that fleeting moment during his makeover when he'd felt like an emerging butterfly. He'd not only looked good outside but felt good inside. Now he doubted whether he'd ever really looked good. Or had Sal merely made him think that?

On the bus, Toro greeted him sheepishly, apparently still embarrassed about the day before. "'S'up?"

Carlos replied with his own reassuring "'S'up."

Playboy gave them a curious look. "What's up with you two girls?"

Carlos ignored him and gazed out the window, annoyed.

Then Playboy announced, "Last night I dumped BadAssGirl. I

didn't want to be harsh, but I finally told her, 'Look, when I want to hook up, I'll let you know.' So now she says I'm a monster. I am so totally over her. What's up with these girls who want to get laid and then cry hurt? What do they expect?"

Carlos slid down in his bus seat. He couldn't help drawing a parallel with his Roxy experience, except that he was in the role of BadAssGirl. He recalled his dream of turning into a girl and wondered, *Am I actually becoming one?*

At school his stomach churned at the prospect of seeing Roxy. All morning long, he sat at his desk fidgeting, oblivious to his teachers' lectures, trying to adjust his mindset. Why couldn't he simply accept that Roxy and he had hooked up, nothing more, and just be happy with that?

But as he jostled through the crowd toward the lunchroom, he unexpectedly found himself directly behind her. He recognized her blonde-streaked hair and slim figure immediately—except that she wasn't with her girl friends or alone. Her arm was slung around Senior Dude's waist, with his arm draped across her shoulder.

An explosion occurred in Carlos's brain, as a thousand nerve cells fired in every direction. Why didn't Roxy simply rip his heart out and stomp on it with cleats? In the chaos of his feelings, he clenched his fists, wanting to strike Senior Dude, or Roxy, or both of them. And yet his eyes were misting with tears.

"Hey, you okay?" a voice asked beside him. Carlos turned to see Toro, offering a worried smile.

"I don't know," Carlos replied. Inside, he felt like he was breaking down, no longer in control of what he felt or said or did.

"Maybe you'd better sit down," Toro told him. "I'll get your lunch."

He guided Carlos toward Playboy and Pulga, but Carlos didn't feel like eating. He stared across the cafeteria, watching Roxy feed Senior Dude forkfuls of cherry cobbler.

Carlos wanted to shout at her, "You slut!" But his throat felt too clenched to even speak.

For the first time, he thought how he should've listened to Sal's warning about Roxy. He recalled Sal saying he didn't want to see Carlos get hurt. Now that recollection only made Carlos feel crappier about how he'd ditched and lied to Sal—for a girl who'd only wanted to hook up.

His afternoon blurred past as he stared at his books, unable to focus on the words. On the bus ride home Playboy continued to gripe about BadAssGirl: "She's gotten full psycho-needy. Today, she called my cell a million times, boo-hoo-ing, 'Why don't you like me anymore? Boo-hoo-hoo!'" He screwed his fists into his eye sockets as if wiping away tears.

Carlos bristled in his bus seat. Before, he'd always admired Playboy's devil-may-care attitude toward life and girls. What had changed? Or had Playboy always been such a jerk?

"Someone needs to tell these chicks that needy is *not* hot," Playboy continued. "I never told her I liked her in the first place. What part of 'It was just a hookup' doesn't she get?"

Carlos clenched his fists and roared, "Would you shut the hell up?"

He wanted to punch Playboy. But, instead, he got off at the next stop, and seethed all the way home.

Fifty-Eight

CARLOS WAS STILL feeling cranky that evening when Raúl came over for his usual midweek visit. After dinner, Carlos did some homework.

Once again, he tried to ignore the sound of squeaking bedsprings, except that he couldn't use his headphones. They remained broken, and his ma hadn't given him any money for new ones. Now, a wave of anger engulfed him.

He got up and locked his bedroom door, switched on his stereo, and loaded a CD. Then he cranked the volume to the max—louder than he'd ever dared to play it. A blast of Los Lonely Boys shook the walls, obliterating the sound of his ma and Raúl.

An instant later, he heard his ma's muted shouting beneath the bass beat. "Carlos! Turn that down!" The doorknob jiggled. "Open this door, right now!"

"Carlos!" Raúl echoed, pounding on his door. "What's the matter with you?"

Carlos's heartbeat quickened. He knew there was no key, so what could they do besides shout? Break the door down?

He waited, tense and excited, till eventually his ma and Raúl gave up yelling. By then, his ears were ringing. The music was too loud even for him. He turned off the stereo and climbed into bed, exhausted. At least it was quiet now—no more bedsprings.

The following morning, Raúl had already left for work when Carlos walked into the kitchen. His ma sat at the breakfast table, glaring at him. "Sit down," she ordered.

"I'm hungry," Carlos protested, pulling the cereal box from the cupboard.

His ma leaped up and yanked the box away. "I said, sit down!" Her voice screeched angrier than ever. "We're going to talk."

Carlos dropped into the chair opposite her. "About what?"

"You know what!" His ma crossed her arms. "About last night. What was that all about?"

Carlos slouched down in his chair. "I'd told you that my headphones broke. You didn't give me any money. I wanted to listen to my music."

"Carlos!" His ma unfolded her arms, throwing them in the air. "The neighbors nearly called the police. You could hear the music three doors away."

Carlos pressed his lips together to keep from smiling.

"You think it's funny?" His ma's eyebrows shot up.

"Kind of." It felt good to tell her the truth.

"Well, I don't," his ma hissed. "What's going on, *mi'jo*?" Her tone softened into one of concern. "This isn't like you."

Carlos shifted in his chair, his guard beginning to waver. "My headphones broke. I told you that."

"So you decided to let the entire neighborhood know?" His ma's forehead crisscrossed in frustration. "No, there's more to this. Tell me. I want to know. What's going on?"

Carlos leaned back in his chair. Did he have the nerve to tell her? He gripped the table, took a deep breath, and said in a low voice, "I can hear you."

His ma stared at Carlos, her eyes blank with confusion. "What?"

Carlos glanced away, his face warming like an oven, as he choked out the words: "When Raúl comes over, I can hear you in your bedroom."

His ma sat silently, and Carlos gazed up at her. Her cheeks flushed with embarrassment as she whispered, "Why didn't you say anything?"

Carlos whispered back through gritted teeth, "I shouldn't *have* to say anything." As he spoke he felt his chin start quivering, and he had to hold his breath to keep from choking up. "Either marry him or go somewhere else. I don't like hearing you."

His eyes clouded with tears that he didn't want to be there. It made him feel like a kid. But he couldn't stop them. His chest heaved, and the teardrops rolled down his cheeks.

His ma stepped around the table to him. And when she wrapped her arms around him, he let them stay there.

Fifty-Nine

By TALKING TO his ma about her and Raúl, Carlos felt like a weight the size of a school bus had been hoisted off his shoulders. As he walked to his bus stop, he recalled Sal's encouraging him to open up. Now, Carlos wished he'd done so earlier.

But the cry also left him feeling exposed, even with his jean jacket on—as though his skin were barely holding him together. When he boarded the bus, he stared out the window, barely speaking to his buds.

"What's your problem?" Playboy asked. "You still on the rag?"

Carlos ignored him, as Pulga announced to the group, "I went to Carlotta's last night for dinner—and met her mom." He gazed at Carlos, a tiny, proud smile playing at the edges of his mouth.

"Whoa, whoa, whoa!" Playboy raised his arms in protest. "I thought she'd dumped your sorry little ass."

Pulga's expression turned guarded. "I want to get back together . . . even if it means having to be her boyfriend."

Toro nodded sympathetically, but Playboy flicked his wrist as if cracking a whip.

"Meow." He leaned into Pulga. "Pussy-whipped! Pussy-whipped!"

"Up yours!" Pulga aimed a punch at his shoulder, but Playboy grabbed hold of his arms, chanting, "Pussy-whipped! Pussy-whipped!"

"Lay off him," Carlos said, but Playboy pinned Pulga against the seat, howling, "Pussy-whipped! Pussy-whipped!"

"Leave him alone!" Carlos exploded. He swung out to punch Playboy on the shoulder, like they always did to each other, but his fist slipped—and hit Playboy's chin.

Playboy whirled around, his eyes burning. He released Pulga. Then his fist slammed into Carlos's eye.

A bolt of pain seared through Carlos's face. He lashed back, the blood pounding in his ears.

"Fight! Fight!" the other students shouted.

The next thing Carlos knew, Playboy and he were scuffling on the bus floor, while Toro tried to pry them apart. The engine came to a stop and the driver shoved through the crush of students. A multitude of hands pulled the boys away from each other. The driver grabbed Carlos by the jacket collar and ordered him to sit up front in the seat beside Vicky.

"But he's the one who went crazy!" Carlos jabbed a finger toward Playboy.

The driver plopped Carlos into an empty seat. His eye throbbed with pain.

Vicky cringed at the sight of him. "Here!" She handed Carlos a tissue from her backpack. "You'd better put some ice on that when we get to school."

He dabbed his eye and watched the tissue smear red with blood. It seemed unreal how fast everything had happened. Had one of his best friends actually pounded him? They'd never hurt each other like that before.

The driver radioed the school about the fight. When they arrived, the school police officer was waiting.

She escorted Carlos and Playboy through the hallway toward the main office. Students gaped and winced at Carlos's face, making him wonder how bad he must look. Meanwhile, Playboy, largely unscathed, grinned proudly.

Carlos felt stupid for his part in starting the fight, but at least he'd gotten Playboy to shut up and leave Pulga alone.

The vice principal for discipline was at some meeting, so, once again, Carlos had to face Hard-Ass Harris.

"I didn't mean to hit him," Carlos explained. "My hand slipped."

"Yeah, my hand slipped too," Playboy's voice echoed with sarcasm.

"I won't tolerate fighting." Harris scowled. "Especially on a bus." He made a long speech about how disappointed he was in both of them, and how he hoped this was an "aberration," blah, blah, blah . . . After sentencing them both to a week of after-school detention, to start the following day, he dismissed both boys, ordering Carlos to the infirmary.

When he saw his reflection in the nurse's mirror, Carlos cringed. The white part of his left eye was streaked red. Below the eyelid, his cheek was swollen like a puffy black mushroom, oozing blood. No wonder it hurt so much.

The nurse dabbed on some disinfectant, which made the wound smart even more. Then she made him phone his ma. When he told her about the fight and his detention, she sort of had a nuclear meltdown.

"You've never acted like this!" she screamed into the phone. "What is happening to you?"

Carlos remained silent, unable to explain.

Later, at home, she continued her rant as she prepared an ice pack for him. "This weekend, you're seeing your father, whether you want to or not."

Oh, great. The last thing Carlos felt like was a lecture from his so-called father. "Why do I have to see *him*?"

"Because!" His ma handed Carlos the ice pack. "I'm not going to have you turn into a delinquent."

Carlos rolled his eyes. Getting into a fight with Playboy made him a delinquent?

"I'm not going," Carlos muttered, pressing the cold pack against this cheek. "*You* never want to see him—why should I?"

His ma stared coldly back at Carlos. In spite of his protests, she phoned his pa. After telling him what had happened, she passed the phone to Carlos.

He didn't want to take it, but she looked hostile enough to smack him a second black eye if he didn't.

His pa's voice was stern. "You're coming with me on Saturday."

"No, I'm not," Carlos mumbled. He wasn't going back to being treated like a kid, forced to spend time with his toddler stepbrother and the woman who'd broken up his family.

"You're coming!" his pa retorted, and hung up.

The rest of the week sucked more than ever. During classes, Carlos couldn't concentrate. At detention, he slouched behind a desk like the other "delinquents." And at lunchtime, he barely ate, watching Roxy feed Senior Creep forkfuls of peach tart.

In general, Carlos steered clear of Playboy, who also did the same. At lunch, they barely spoke. And on the morning bus, they sat on opposite sides of the back row, with Pulga and Toro as a buffer between them. Yet, even though Carlos remained pissed at Playboy for the black eye, he also felt weirdly relieved. The fight had released something long-simmering in their relationship, though Carlos couldn't exactly describe what.

In the evenings, Carlos retreated to his once-again-chaotic bedroom, examining his bruised eye in the mirror as it gradually turned from black to purple. Or he lay in bed, staring up at the empty space where the praying mantis had hung.

Saturday at noon, his pa cell-phoned from his car downstairs, but Carlos remained lying on his bed, refusing to answer. His pulse quickened with anxiety as his ma stormed into the bedroom doorway. "Carlos, get up! You're going with your father!"

"No, I'm not!" He shook his head resolutely.

"Yes, you are!"

"No! I'm not!"

The doorbell rang. His ma whirled around and stamped out of his room.

Carlos sat up, his heart racing. Would she actually let his pa into their apartment for the first time since the divorce? A moment later, he heard the front door open, followed by heated arguing. Not only were his parents talking more than in the entire past three years, but his ma had actually let his pa into their home again.

Hearing their approach, Carlos laid back down, summoning every fiber in his body to feign calm.

Sixty

AFTER WEEKS OF not seeing his pa, what struck Carlos most was how small he looked. *Am I still growing?* Carlos wondered.

"That's quite a shiner." His pa peered across the room at his bruised eye.

Carlos averted his gaze, unwilling to let his guard down, even though it felt good to see his pa and ma talking side by side again.

"What's the problem, *mi'jo?*" his pa asked.

"No problem." Carlos strained to keep his voice steady. "I told you, I don't want to go."

"And *I* told *you*, you're coming. Now, put your shoes on."

Carlos folded his arms across his chest, refusing to budge, while his heart nearly galloped out of his throat.

"See?" his ma told his pa. "He won't listen! And he's getting into fights."

"It was an accident!" Carlos barked.

"*Calma!*" His pa turned to his ma. "Let me talk to him alone."

"You'd better listen to your father!" His ma shook her finger at Carlos and stomped out.

His pa sat down in the desk chair, eyeing Carlos warily. "You know, you've upset your mother very much."

Carlos sneered. "Since when do you care about her anymore?"

His pa shot him a sharp look. "I *do* care."

"Yeah, right."

"Look, what happened between your ma and me is between her and me."

A surge of anger swelled in Carlos's chest, rising into his throat. "And what about *me*?"

His pa frowned, refusing to meet Carlos's eyes. Then he glanced at his watch. "*Mi'jo,* we have to go. Lupita and Henry are waiting in the car."

"That's not my fault," Carlos growled. "I told you I didn't want to go."

His pa tapped his foot impatiently. "Why don't you want to come?"

"Because it's boring! We always do the same thing—take Henry to McDonald's, take Henry to the park, rent a movie for Henry . . ."

His pa stared down at his hands as if thinking. "Henry's my son, same as you."

"Then how come everything is always about *him*?"

His pa's gaze moved carefully up and across Carlos's face. "What do you want?"

Carlos knew what he wanted to say, but why should he have to say it? The image of Sal flashed across his mind, and Carlos recalled the day Javier had told Carlos, "If you don't tell him, how will he know?"

Now, Carlos felt the emotion bubble up inside him. His voice cracked painfully. "Can't we do something . . . just you and me . . . like we used to?"

Two big tears rolled down his cheeks. Quickly, he turned over on the bed, not wanting his pa to see his face. He'd probably call Carlos a *maricón* again. Was that part of why he'd felt so ashamed to tell his pa how much he missed him? Because it was considered *gay* for a guy to express his feelings for another guy?

His pa cleared his throat, nervous-like. "Okay," he said softly. "It *has* been a while since you and I spent time, just the two of us."

Carlos rolled back over to face him, no longer so embarrassed by his tears. As he gazed into his pa's eyes he noticed that they looked a

little wet too, brimming with a sadness he'd never seen in them
before.

Carlos put on his sneakers, then tugged on his denim jacket and
followed his pa to the living room. His ma was waiting, sitting on the
edge of the couch.

"Good!" She rose to her feet at the sight of Carlos. "Now, listen to
your father. And no more fights. Understand?"

"He'll be fine," his pa told her. "He's just learning to stand up for
himself."

Carlos assumed his pa was referring to the fight with Playboy. Or
did his pa mean standing up *to him*?

The three of them stood silently for a moment, looking at each
other, and Carlos wondered if his pa and ma were thinking the same
thought: *Why did all this have to happen? Why couldn't we be a family
again?*

His pa shuffled his feet and told Carlos, "We'd better go."

True to his word, after lunch his pa dropped off Lupita and Henry
at their home and asked Carlos, "So, what would you like to do?"

"I don't know." Carlos hadn't thought that far ahead. "Can we just
drive around some?"

His pa nodded and drove toward Town Lake. Neither of them
really said much. It almost felt like they were strangers, rather than
father and son.

"Your ma mentioned a girl you're seeing," his pa said at last. "Is she
a girlfriend?"

It was the first time in hours that Carlos had thought about Roxy.
"No," he muttered.

His pa responded with a knowing look. "I forgot how hard it can be
at your age. Women can be pretty confusing." He shook his head and
gave a little snort. "Even at my age."

Carlos squirmed in his seat, a little surprised. His pa had always sounded like an expert on women. Now, as Carlos gazed at the road ahead, his mind filled with doubts. If his pa couldn't get his act together at *his* age, how could Carlos ever hope to? Was he also destined to be confused by women all his life?

His pa parked the car beside the lakeside park where they'd caught insects when Carlos was little. But, this time, they didn't stop for bugs.

As they walked down a trail, Carlos thought how many questions he wished his pa could answer: about why Roxy had wanted to hook up but didn't want to be his girlfriend; about why he got so flustered around girls; about why his pa had gotten involved with Lupita . . . Immersed in his thoughts, Carlos strode ahead, unaware that he was leaving his pa behind.

"*Mi'jo,* slow down!"

Carlos stopped and his pa strode up, a little short of breath. Then Carlos began walking again, a little slower.

"That was nice," his pa told Carlos when he drove him home to drop him off. "Let's do it again soon, *mi'jo.*"

He wrapped his arm around Carlos's shoulder. For a second, Carlos resisted the embrace—the first he'd gotten from his pa in weeks—but then he relaxed. Even if his pa couldn't give him the answers he longed for, at least for a change he hadn't had to share him with Henry and Lupita.

"*Te quiero,*" his pa whispered, and Carlos answered, "Love you too."

He watched the car drive off until it disappeared around the corner. Then he bounded up the stairway.

Inside the apartment, Raúl was on the couch, watching TV. He waved to Carlos. "Hey, want to watch the game with me?"

Carlos sat down, still happy about his pa. But his stomach began to clench as he wondered: Would Raúl spend the night again?

All evening, Carlos waited, but Raúl never entered his ma's bedroom. After dinner, TV, and the ten o'clock news, Raúl kissed Carlos's ma good night, waved to Carlos, and headed home.

Carlos channel-surfed as his ma planted a kiss on his forehead. "Don't stay up too late, okay?"

Carlos stared at the TV and thought back over the events of the past few days: his arguments with his ma and pa, and how he'd finally told them the stuff he'd been holding inside; how he was finally learning to open up and stand up for himself; and how so much of it was thanks to Sal.

On impulse, he picked up the phone and dialed Sal's number, though he wasn't exactly certain what to say if Sal answered. His palms began to sweat while the phone rang about a million times. Was Sal screening his number? Finally, the line rolled to voice mail.

"Hey, it's Carlos. Call me, okay?" He was about to hang up when he added, "Please?"

Then he shut off the TV and headed toward bed.

Sixty-One

LATE SUNDAY MORNING, Carlos had barely woken up when Pulga called: "Hey, *pendejo,* you want to go to the mall?"

Before Carlos could answer, his call-waiting clicked. "Hold on," he told Pulga and switched lines. "Hello?"

"Hey," Toro said. "I've been thinking about . . . you know . . . I want to tell Pulga about me. Will you help me do it?"

Carlos sat up in bed, grinning at the coincidence. "Sure. He's on the other line. Want me to conference him in?"

"No!" Toro shouted in panic. "Are you crazy?"

"Just kidding." Carlos tried to calm him down. "He wants to go to the mall. You want to go?"

He heard Toro catch his breath. "Okay. But you promise to help me?"

"Yeah," Carlos assured him. "Come on over."

He switched to Pulga's line. "Toro's coming. You want to meet here?"

After hanging up, Carlos walked to the bathroom and peered in the mirror. As he examined his bruised eye—now mostly a barfy yellow color—it struck Carlos how neither of his buds had mentioned inviting Playboy. Maybe Pulga didn't want Playboy hassling him because of Carlotta. And Toro probably wasn't ready to come out to Playboy. Or maybe Pulga and Toro were afraid Carlos and Playboy might get into another fight.

As it happened, both Toro and Pulga arrived at the same time.

"What happened to your room?" Toro asked. "It looks like a dump again."

True, Carlos thought, and it was starting to get on his nerves. "Can you guys help me clean it up?"

Pulga chuckled. "How much will you pay us?"

It was good to hear him kidding. He'd started joking a lot more again, ever since getting back together with Carlotta and agreeing to be a real couple.

The boys started to pick up Carlos's stuff when Toro's phone rang. He pulled the cell from his pocket and glanced at the number. "It's Playboy."

Carlos expected Toro would answer it, but Toro let the phone ring, gazing at Carlos and Pulga, as though waiting for them to say something. But they merely stared at Toro, listening till the cell stopped ringing.

"Should I call him back?" Toro whispered. His eyes darted guiltily between Pulga and Carlos.

"If you want." Carlos shrugged. "It's up to you."

"He shouldn't have smacked you like that." Pulga shook his head at Carlos.

Toro nodded in agreement. "He's changed."

"No." Carlos gave a sigh. "He's the same as he's always been. *We're* the ones who've changed."

The three boys gazed at one another. Then Toro slipped the phone back into his pocket, and no one said another word about Playboy's call.

The boys helped Carlos throw out trash, return dirty dishes to the kitchen, and lug his stinky clothes to the laundry room.

"Wait!" he told his buds as they loaded the washers. "You've got to separate colors and whites."

"Really?" Pulga said. "Sure you're not turning into a fag?" He registered the angry expression on Carlos's face and added, "Hey, just joking."

Carlos continued scowling. "Even kidding, don't use the word 'fag.' Okay?"

He glanced at Toro, whose ears glowed red as he too spoke up: "Um, yeah . . . ," he stammered at Pulga. "I don't like it either."

Pulga peered at him, curious-like, then broke into a grin. "Well, we already know you're gay."

Toro shot a vexed look at Carlos, but Carlos defended himself. "I didn't tell him."

Pulga raised his eyebrows. "Tell me what?"

Toro's eyes darted between Carlos and Pulga. Carlos gave him an encouraging nod. Toro swallowed a noticeable lump in his throat, and told Pulga: "I'm gay."

Pulga stared at him, his jaw dropping open, then he turned to Carlos.

Carlos wanted to say something supportive to Toro, who looked so exposed and vulnerable, he almost seemed ready to cry. But Carlos also sensed that he needed to let Toro stand up for himself.

"But—but . . . ," Pulga stuttered. "What about Leticia?"

Toro glanced down at the concrete floor of the laundry room. "I made her up."

"You *what*?" Pulga shook his head. "Why didn't you just tell us the truth?"

Toro's voice trembled like a child's. "I was afraid you guys wouldn't like me anymore."

Pulga was silent for a seemingly endless moment. Then he gave a sigh of resignation. Slowly, a smile played across his lips. "And what makes you think we ever liked you in the first place? " He reached up and gave Toro a punch on the shoulder. "Well, since you're officially gay, you've got to help me shop."

"Huh?" Little by little, the corners of Toro's downcast mouth turned up, as the acceptance implied in Pulga's words slowly dawned on him. "Okay! What do you need to buy?"

Pulga gave a sheepish shrug. "A birthday present for Carlotta."

"But didn't her birthday pass already?" Carlos asked.

"Yeah, but . . . I know it'll make her happy."

Carlos and his buds nodded at one another. After the laundry was dry and folded, they walked to the mall in search of perfume for Carlotta.

"Would you guys mind if she sat with us at lunch?" Pulga asked. "She's been bugging me about that."

"I don't mind." Carlos abruptly spritzed him with perfume.

"Fine with me." Toro ambushed Pulga from the other side.

"Hey, cut it out, *pendejos!*" Pulga grabbed a perfume bottle, spraying them back.

All afternoon they joked and clowned around, closer than ever. It was like they'd opened up and now knew each other in ways they never had. And Carlos felt happier than he had in the last three years—except for one thing.

When he got back home, he asked his ma if Sal had called him back from the night before. He hadn't.

Sixty-Two

MONDAY MORNING, CARLOS woke up determined to talk to Sal. He couldn't take one more day of keeping inside what he wanted to tell him, even if Sal refused to respond.

After lunch, Carlos scanned the hallway. Among the crowd he spotted a bright magenta shirt and shiny hoop earrings. "Sal!" Carlos ran past the other students to catch up to him. "Can I talk to you a minute? Please?"

Sal stopped and turned, but his eyes were hard and his mouth was a flat, unsmiling line.

Carlos wanted to go somewhere the whole school wouldn't see them and hear what he wished to say. But what if that suggestion made Sal walk away like before? Not wanting to risk it, Carlos took a breath. "Look, I'm sorry I bagged out on the GSA meeting."

In response, Sal stared at him, not saying a word.

Carlos strained against the tightness in his throat. "And that I lied to you about it."

Sal gazed away, still not answering, and Carlos began to feel like an idiot. He thought how nothing felt stupider than when someone wouldn't talk back, making anything you said sound ridiculous— especially in front of other people.

"Are you ever going to talk to me?" Carlos pleaded.

Sal flashed him the briefest glance. It was only for a second, but at least it confirmed he was listening.

Encouraged, Carlos pressed on. "It's one of the dumbest things

I've ever done. I wish I could undo it, but I can't. So, can we at least be friends?"

He waited, no longer caring that almost every student in school was walking past, seeing him practically begging Sal.

Sal must've been aware of what Carlos was feeling. He watched the passing crowd, gave a long, thoughtful sigh, and returned his gaze to Carlos. "I don't know if being friends can work."

That was all he said. And without another word, he turned and walked away.

Carlos stood amid the stream of students, his thoughts swirling, and shouted, "Can't we at least try?"

He thought he saw Sal pause for a moment, as though reconsidering, but then Sal kept walking, fading into the crowd. The bell rang, and Carlos turned slowly toward class, not caring if he were late.

That afternoon, Carlos's English class went to the library. He sat at the same table where the GSA group had made their posters.

And for the first time since the afternoon he'd ditched the meeting, he let himself fully imagine what it must've felt like for Sal that day: eager and excited to hold the school's first-ever GSA, and then not a single other student from the entire school showed up. Not one.

Sal must've felt totally depressed, like nobody cared. And Carlos recalled Sal's telling him how lonely it had been growing up gay—and no one wanting to be his friend.

Carlos thought about how Sal had helped him, even after Carlos stopped paying him. How Sal had given up his Saturdays for him and encouraged him to speak up to his ma and pa. How Sal had really been the first person in Carlos's life he'd truly opened up to. He thought about all the stuff Sal had taught him and given him, and how, after everything Sal had done for him,

Carlos had ditched him, on the faint chance of getting laid.

Carlos's heart wrenched with shame. He cradled his head on the table and closed his eyes, wishing he could disappear. But he couldn't escape from the glaring truth of what he was: selfish, superficial, and immature, having been more interested in getting his rocks off than keeping his bargain with a friend.

Could he really blame Sal for not wanting to be his friend? Why would *anyone* want to be his friend?

He raised his head off the table and opened his eyes again, hoping to shake off the shame. Staring back from a bookshelf was one of Mr. Quiñones's famous dead-guy quotes:

> *Life contains but two tragedies:*
> *one is not to get your heart's desire;*
> *the other is to get it.*
> —Socrates

To Carlos, it sounded like, either way, you were screwed in life. Given his recent experience, that seemed accurate: He'd nearly gotten Roxy, but he hadn't. And what if he had? She'd turned out to be so very different from what he'd imagined.

Carlos reread the quote, still trying to make sense of it. Something Sal had once said came to mind: *Maybe life isn't about what you get, it's about what you give.*

Carlos wished he could give Sal something, to win his friendship back. But what could he give him? Carlos was broke. Besides, Sal didn't even want to speak to him.

The bell rang and Carlos rose from the library table, still wondering what old Socrates had meant. He collected his books and glanced at the words one last time. Abruptly, he froze. A chill ran through his entire body. Suddenly, he got it.

The tragedies were because life was neither about getting, nor about giving to get something back. Life was simply about giving, even though you might never get anything back. That's what Sal had meant!

And with that realization, Carlos knew the greatest gift he could give Sal.

Sixty-Three

THE FOLLOWING MORNING when Carlos boarded the bus, he asked Vicky, "Can, I, um, sit with you?"

Her brow furrowed with skepticism. "Why?"

The bus lurched forward, bouncing Carlos into the vacant seat. "Look, I want to say I'm sorry about middle school . . . That I stopped being your friend."

"Why did you ditch me like some leper?" Vicky's voice cracked with hurt. "What did I do to you?"

Carlos grew warm beneath his jean jacket. Could he tell Vicky the truth—that he'd ditched her because she'd started dressing weird and he feared being seen with her?

"It was me," he simply said. "I was stupid, okay? I've changed now."

"Oh, *really*?" Vicky's cheeks sank into a smirk. "Then why'd you ditch Sal and the GSA meeting?"

Carlos flushed red, realizing he'd set himself up. "Because I was stupid—*again*. But now I really have changed, and I want to prove it."

Vicky rolled her eyes doubtfully. "How?"

Carlos lowered his voice and ventured his idea. "I want us to organize another GSA meeting."

He'd figured Vicky would be thrilled about it, but instead, she shook her head. "Sal told me he's not doing it. He was really hurt that none of us showed for the meeting—including me." Her mouth drooped, brooding. "We really let him down."

"I know!" Carlos insisted. "That's why we need to do this—even if he doesn't come—to show him *we* believe it's important."

Vicky cocked her head, eyeing Carlos skeptically. "Since when did you get crowned Mr. Social Justice? Besides, what's the point if no one else shows up?"

Carlos gazed out the bus window. "I've been thinking about that. Maybe part of the problem was having the meeting after school, when people have too much other stuff to do—you know, sports, other clubs—"

"Detention?" Vicky needled him.

Carlos ignored her barb. "The GSA websites say that some groups meet at lunchtime to boost attendance. Why not try that?"

Vicky gave him a hard look. "Will you actually show up this time?"

"Yes!" Carlos said testily. "Come on! Please? I need your help."

"Okay, but . . ." Vicky clenched her fingers into a fist. "If you don't show up this time, I swear, I'll smack you a bigger black eye than Playboy ever could."

Carlos grinned nervously, unsure if she was merely teasing.

As he got off the bus, his sitting with Vicky predictably caused comment from his buds—at least from Playboy. "*Pendejo,* you must really be hard up to get laid!"

Carlos shoved his fists into his pockets, refusing to be goaded into another fight. Over the past few days, he and Playboy had begun speaking to each other again. Neither had apologized, but Carlos was trying to get along, even though it felt awkward.

As Carlos arrived at lunch that day, he was relieved to see a new face sitting at his group's table. Next to Pulga, in Playboy's usual place, sat Carlotta.

Playboy now sat on the opposite side of the table, looking crankily displaced.

"Hi, Carlos!" Carlotta waved cheerfully. "Thanks for helping Pulga choose the perfume. I love it!"

"Sure," Carlos replied, sitting beside Toro.

As the boys ate lunch, it became apparent how much the presence of a girl changed the tone. No one burped or mentioned boobs. In fact, none of the guys seemed sure what to say.

But Carlotta spoke up. "Vicky says you want to try starting the GSA again," she told Carlos. "Count me in!"

"Okay." Carlos smiled back, pretending not to notice Playboy's scowl.

Carlotta turned to Pulga. "I want you to come too."

Playboy redirected his frown at Pulga and uttered a single word: "Meow."

Carlotta flashed a glance at Playboy. "What's 'meow' mean?"

Playboy grinned diabolically. "Ask Pulga."

Pulga squirmed in his chair, glaring at Playboy, and turned to face Carlotta. He seemed so tiny compared to her. "Why should I go to the GSA? I'm not gay."

"Yes, you've proven that." She rolled her eyes. "It's a Gay-*Straight* Alliance. Come on, it'll be fun!"

Toro abruptly cleared his throat and announced, "Um, I'll go."

"What's this turning into?" Playboy sputtered in disgust. "The fag-lover table?"

Everyone turned silent. Carlos noticed a thin band of perspiration beading on Toro's forehead.

"The word is 'gay.'" Toro turned to Playboy. "Not 'fag.'"

"Oh, yeah?" Playboy picked up his burger. "Well, go to that meeting and people will think *you're* one."

Toro sat up calmly, his muscled frame filling the chair, as though he'd anticipated this moment. "And what if I am?"

Playboy dropped his burger as if thunderstruck. Then his gaze shifted left and right, staring at the others. It was the first time that Carlos recalled ever seeing him taken aback by anything. His face seemed to say, *Didn't you guys hear what Toro said? Why are you staring at me and not at him?* Then his jaw clenched, as if he'd realized he was the only one troubled by Toro's announcement.

An instant later, Playboy wordlessly picked up his tray. Without anyone's protesting, he abandoned the group and crossed the cafeteria to sit at another table.

Toro murmured, "I was afraid of that."

"Should I go talk to him?" Pulga asked, but when no one answered him, he stayed seated.

Although the group remained a little somber for the remainder of lunch, Carlos thought how, all things considered, everything was actually turning out pretty well: Toro had come out, Pulga and Carlotta were back together, and everybody in the GSA had agreed to reattempt getting it started—*almost* everyone.

As Carlos exited the cafeteria, he searched for the orange hoodie of one other person he still needed to talk to.

Sixty-Four

ACROSS THE SCHOOL hallway, Carlos called out to Espie, "'S'up?"

She spun around, smiling from beneath her orange sweatshirt. "Oh, hi."

"Um, hi," Carlos said, breaking into an instant sweat.

"Hi," Espie repeated, making Carlos wonder: *Is she nervous too?*

Carlos took a deep breath, trying to bolster his courage. "Um, listen, we're going to try to start the GSA again. You interested?"

"Sure!" Espie beamed, her smile more beautiful than he'd remembered. In fact, the whole rest of her—even in the baggie orange hoodie—looked cuter too.

"Are we going to make posters again?" she asked.

Carlos hadn't thought that far ahead. "Um, I guess so."

Even though their previous posters had gotten defaced and torn down, the group still needed some way to get the word out.

"Okay," Espie said merrily. "I'm there! Got to get to class. See you later!"

And with that, she vanished from sight, but not from Carlos's mind. All afternoon, he thought of her, even forgetting what had happened at lunch—Toro coming out and Playboy ditching the group's table—until it came time to ride home.

Carlos had completed his after-school detention sentence and was back to riding his regular bus. But when he boarded, he found that Playboy had invited some other guys into the last row. Pulga and Toro had switched to those guys' seats halfway toward the front.

"They were already back there when Toro and I got on," Pulga whispered to Carlos.

"What should we do?" Toro asked.

"Nothing," Carlos said thoughtfully. In a way, it seemed like a pretty fair tradeoff: Playboy got the back row of the bus, while Carlos, Pulga, and Toro kept their regular lunch table. In another way, it sucked, reminding him of his parents' divorce.

Arriving home, Carlos gazed at the mirror photo of "Los Horny Boys" standing beside the roller coaster on his thirteenth birthday. Apart from his family, the guys had been the people closest to him for nearly half his life. Their ringleader, Playboy, had been one of their best friends.

Why couldn't Playboy now accept how Pulga, Toro, and Carlos had changed—and change along with them?

Yet, Carlos realized that, for whatever reason, Playboy wouldn't. Turning away from the photo, his chest felt empty with grief, as he slowly let out a breath.

That evening at dinner, his ma passed him a serving dish full of green beans. "I want to discuss something," she announced. "Raúl and I have been talking. How would you feel about him and me getting married?"

The question shouldn't have surprised Carlos: he'd asked her about it before. But this time *she'd* brought it up. It took a moment for him to sort his feelings. What would it feel like to have Raúl as his stepdad? He'd have to ask his ma to get a quieter bed. But, apart from that, there wasn't anything that majorly annoyed Carlos about the guy—and he wanted his ma to be happy.

Raising his glass of water, he told her, "It's about time!"

Later that week, Carlos, Pulga, Toro, and Carlotta met in the library during lunch to make the GSA posters, together with Vicky and Espie.

"This time," Espie suggested, "why don't we try targeting straight students? Maybe that way, the signs won't get torn down so fast."

"Good idea," everyone agreed, and Vicky came up with a poster that read:

> STRAIGHT BUT NOT NARROW?
> JOIN THE GAY-*STRAIGHT* ALLIANCE

Carlotta wrote another:

> IT'S *NOT* A GAY CLUB,
> IT'S A PLACE FOR *ALL* STUDENTS

And Carlos thought up one that said:

> HOMOPHOBIA HURTS STRAIGHT PEOPLE TOO
> FIND OUT WHAT YOU CAN DO

When the group split up to post the signs, Pulga naturally went with Carlotta, and Toro volunteered to go with Vicky. That left Espie with Carlos.

His legs wobbled nervously as they walked down the quiet hallway. Sweat burst from his pores, prickling his skin. He racked his brain for something to say, but he came up blank. When they stopped to put up their first poster, Carlos lifted the sign while Espie handed him the tape, smiling at him from beneath her sweatshirt hood.

"You're really cute," he blurted without thinking. "You shouldn't hide beneath your hoodie."

The color sprang into his cheeks and Espie gave a nervous giggle. "Thanks. My mom is always telling me that. But without it, I feel sort of—you know—naked?"

Carlos wished she hadn't said "naked." The word set off a pair of boobs dancing through his brain. "Here." He pulled off his denim jacket. "Wear this instead."

"Your jacket?"

"Yeah." He held it out to her, hardly believing his boldness. But he also felt weirdly like he didn't need the jacket anymore.

Espie gave him a curious grin. Then she pulled off her sweatshirt, handed it to him, and slipped into the jacket. "How's it look?"

"Good." Even though the jacket was a little big, Carlos liked seeing her in it.

They resumed walking down the hall, and he realized he was no longer sweating or forgetting how to speak. He found himself telling her about his bug collection, music, and anything else that popped into his mind. Espie listened as though truly interested. At this rate, who knew what could happen in the future? At some point he might actually work up the nerve to ask her out—not for a hookup, but for a *real* date. And maybe, he'd even someday, finally, have a girlfriend.

Later that week at lunch, Carlos got the uneasy feeling that someone was staring at him. He gazed across the cafeteria toward the table where Roxy sat—just in time to see her glance away.

It was the first time in days she'd looked anywhere near his direction. And Carlos noticed, too, that Senior Dude was missing from her group.

What had happened? Had Roxy chewed up the dude and spit him out like she had Carlos? Or had the guy dumped her? And in spite of everything, a little voice in Carlos asked. *Does that mean I stand another chance with her?*

The response came that evening, when an IM arrived from GlitterGirl: *U wanna hook up? I promise my mom won't be home till late.*☺ *Wanna?*

Carlos sat up in his chair. Did Roxy's message mean she still liked him—or whatever it was she'd felt toward him?

His mind flashed to images of making out on her sofa. Inside his pants, he stirred with excitement, ready to bolt out the door. And yet he stopped himself. Did he really want to hook up again with a girl who had crushed his heart and pretty much totaled him?

His fingers sprang onto the keyboard and typed, *Yes.*

But when he moved to hit send, he hesitated. Was the chance of getting laid worth the risk of Roxy's hurting him again? Besides, what about the possibility of dating someone who seemed a lot more genuine, like Espie? Wasn't that what he really wanted?

He drew a measured breath and hit the backspace key, slowly erasing the *s* . . . the *e* . . . and the *y*. In their place he wrote, *Can't. Sorry.* He politely added *Thanks*, like Sal had taught him. And then: *Goodbye.*

After sending the message, he deleted Roxy from his buddy list. Then he collapsed onto his bed, exhausted—and strangely at peace.

Sixty-Five

AT SCHOOL IN the following days, each time Carlos walked down the hallway, he expected to see the GSA posters once again marked up or torn down. But they weren't. Apparently, Espie's idea of messages directed to and for straight people had worked. Or maybe people had simply lost interest.

"The real test," Carlotta said at lunch, "will be if any new people actually show up."

In addition to new faces, Carlos wondered about somebody else, but Vicky dampened his hopes. "I tried convincing Sal he should come, but he's still too mad at us. I told him he's being a drama queen."

Carlos nodded, masking his disappointment. But secretly, he still hoped.

The morning of the meeting, he awoke well before his alarm, his arteries pumping with anticipation—and anxiety. Since resurrecting the GSA had been his idea, the group had elected him to lead it.

When the lunch bell rang, he headed directly toward the library, too nervous to grab anything to eat. He paused only to duck into the boys' rest room. Peering into the scratched-up mirror, he once again took a long, hard look at himself. The image staring back surprised him: neither a hopeless loser nor a phony, made-over stud. He was simply Carlos Amoroso, a *pendejo* at times, but mostly just a typical teenage boy trying to become a man.

He drew himself up and stepped outside. In the hall he caught up with Espie, who was wearing his jean jacket.

"Hi!" She grinned. "Are you nervous?"

"Um, a little." His voice quavered.

She took hold of his hand, giving it a squeeze. And to his amazement, it didn't send him into a breathless, stammering panic. Instead, it reassured him—at least somewhat.

"Hi, vanguards," Mr. Quiñones greeted them as they entered the library. Carlos didn't know what he meant, but he was too nervous to ask.

Pulga, Carlotta, Toro, and Vicky were already there, helping to set up refreshments.

"How about if you guys gather chairs into a circle?" Mr. Quiñones suggested to Carlos and Espie.

"How many do you think we'll need?" Espie asked.

"Um, I don't know," Carlos replied. "Maybe a dozen?"

While they slid chairs across the carpet, Principal Harris strode in, barking something into his walkie-talkie. He positioned himself like an Army MP, poised to shut the meeting down if anybody mentioned the forbidden word: *S-E-X*.

The door squeaked open and two girls slunk in, giggling. One of them, wearing a T-shirt with a sequin heart, whispered to Espie, "Is this the you-know-what group?"

"Yeah, hi. Help yourself to some cookies."

The girls shuffled over to the soft drinks and snacks, looking ready to sneak out if no one else showed up.

"Do you want a cookie?" Espie asked Carlos.

"Um, no thanks." His stomach was still too much a knot.

Another two girls strode in. They were followed by a girl with a jocky-looking boy who mumbled hi to Toro. Two more boys wandered in and nervously veered toward the refreshments. One of them accidentally spilled a Coke, but Mr. Quiñones calmly cleaned it up.

Every time the door squeaked open, Carlos glanced over, hoping it might be Sal. Each time, he was disappointed.

Meanwhile, Pulga and Carlotta pulled more chairs over, widening the circle. Six more students came in. Carlos wiped the sweat from his forehead. Although he was glad that new faces were showing up, he'd never imagined having to speak in front of so many people.

Toro and Vicky scrambled for more chairs, while the new guys pulled tables back to make more room for the growing circle. Soon there were twenty students, then thirty. With each new addition, people seemed to grow more at ease—whereas Carlos was starting to panic.

Espie must've sensed it, because she patted his arm and whispered, "You'll do great."

To his relief, only a few more people came, making the total thirty-three.

"You'd better get started," Mr. Quiñones said.

Carlos glanced at the clock, his heart sinking. If Sal was coming, wouldn't he have gotten here by now?

He took a deep breath and called out, "Everyone? 'S'up? We need to start." He figured the group would ignore him, but, miraculously, everybody turned quiet.

"Um . . ." He blanked for a minute, his thoughts spinning. But then he looked at Pulga and Toro, their eyes brimming with admiration, while Carlotta, Vicky, and Espie smiled encouragement.

Carlos swallowed hard and continued. "The, um, purpose of this group is to . . . raise awareness about homophobia and, um, build understanding . . ."

As he spoke, the door squeaked open again. One last student entered, wearing a bright pink shirt, shiny hoop earrings, and a pair of jeans Carlos recalled once having worn himself.

The boy gazed around, joined the circle, and, for the first time in weeks, smiled forgivingly at Carlos. And with that gesture, all the tension seemed to leave Carlos's body.

"Whether you're gay, straight, or bi," he told the group, "we're glad you're here."

Although he said it to include everyone, most of all he was saying it to Sal.

Glossary of Spanish words not translated in the text

adios: good-bye
caca: poop or doo-doo
calma: calm
gracias: thank you or thanks
mi amor: my love
mi'jo: my son (contraction)
nada: nothing
numero uno: number one
¿por qué?: why?
pulga: flea
¿qué pasó?: what happened?
te quiero: I love you/I care about you

DON'T MISS **THE GOD BOX**

BY ALEX SANCHEZ
NOW AVAILABLE

1

SEX AND RELIGION DON'T MIX,"

MY GRANDMA ONCE TOLD ME. "THE CHURCH SHOULD STAY
OUT OF PEOPLE'S PANTS."

That random memory flashed through my mind the first
morning of senior year, as I tugged my red rubber WHAT
WOULD JESUS DO? wristband—*snap!*—against my wrist. I hoped
the sting would help me forget the sex dream that had woken
me. But it didn't.

I climbed from bed, hurried through my Bible reading and
prayers, then raced through my shower, all the while trying to
stop thinking about the dream.

When I arrived at homeroom, my girlfriend, Angie, had
already snagged us a couple of seats together. She'd been my
best friend since kindergarten, when my family moved from
Mexico to Texas. Now I surprised her with the latest CD of
one of our favorite Christian rock bands.

"No way!" Her bright brown eyes gazed up at me like I was
the only one in her world. "You're so awesome. Thanks!"

While she scanned the CD's song list, I glanced up. A lanky boy I'd never seen before stepped through the doorway. Tiny hoops pierced both ears and his left eyebrow—surprising for our conservative little west Texas town, where even a single earring could get a guy accused of "going gay." His black wavy hair and cedar skin hinted he was most likely Mexican, and his cinnamon-colored eyes almost pulled me toward him. Who was he?

The boy sauntered toward an empty seat where Jude Maldonado—a ratty guy who came to school mostly to make life hell for everybody—had his dirt-smeared cowboy boots kicked up.

"'Sup?" the new guy asked Jude, friendly-like. "Mind if I sit here?"

"You blind?" Jude sneered. "The seat's taken."

All of homeroom turned to watch as New Boy calmly raised his hands.

"Whoa, easy! Keep your chair."

"Here's a seat," Angie, always the rescuer, called over.

"Thanks." The boy walked over with a broad smile. "My name's Manuel."

"I'm Angie. This is Paul."

"Paul?" Manuel locked onto my eyes, as if peering inside me, with a look that was part mischief and part something else. "Not Pablo?"

"Paul," I said firmly. Although my birth certificate actually did say Pablo, I didn't want to be constantly reminded I was from Mexico. I wanted to be American; I didn't want to be different.

During the remainder of homeroom I tried not to stare at Manuel. What was the strange pull I felt toward him, almost like some force stronger than my own? Did he know me from somewhere? And what was up with those earrings?

Throughout morning classes my thoughts kept returning to him. Nervously, I tugged at my WWJD wristband—a habit I had picked up from a friend who used to bite his fingernails like crazy. In order to quit, he started snapping a rubber band against his wrist whenever he caught himself. The pain of the snap, although merely a sting, had helped him stop. In my case, I hoped the trick would stop my mind from thinking things I didn't want to think.

When the lunch bell rang, I eagerly headed to the cafetoria. My lunch group consisted of Angie and two other girls, Dakota and Elizabeth, who were as opposite as hot and cold. Dakota was gangly and tall, with curls of fiery red hair flaring all over the place; she was editor of the school newspaper, Honor Society president, and flexibly progressive. In contrast, Elizabeth was Barbie-doll petite and impeccably blonde, a cheerleader, student council vice president, and adamantly conservative.

Both were feisty and fiercely opinionated. The big difference between them was that Dakota was warm and never harsh. Elizabeth acted warm, but she could be cold as an icicle. The two of them, Angie, and I had been friends since middle school. We were all smart, ranking in the top ten percent of our class, and we all belonged to our Christ on Campus Bible Club.

For as long as I can remember, my closest friends have always been girls. I'm not sure why. I just found early on that generally girls were more open to telling you what was on their minds and listening to what was on yours. You could talk to them about emotional and spiritual stuff, like why somebody wasn't getting along with someone else, or how a certain song made you want to dance or cry, or how you felt God was calling you to do something.

I had guy friends too, but they tended to be more guarded about venturing into discussions much beyond sports, cars, games, or sex. My Christian guy friends were a bit more open to at least talking about God-related stuff, but even at Bible Club the girls did most of the talking. The few guys who attended mostly lobbed scripture verses as though pitching softballs.

In any case, I didn't mind being the only male at our lunch table. It made me feel special. The girls turned to me for advice. Like today: Elizabeth had fought with her boyfriend, Cliff, because she'd seen him talking with his ex. Angie thought Elizabeth was being too severe. Dakota suggested Elizabeth get more info rather than give him the silent treatment. Elizabeth frowned at their opinions, then asked what I thought.

"Well . . ." I gave a diplomatic shrug. "You really think you should crucify the guy just for talking with somebody?"

Elizabeth frowned at that, too, while Angie glanced across the cafeteria. "Hey, there's Manuel."

She waved and I turned to see the new guy holding his tray, scanning the room for a place to sit.

"Ooh, he's cute. Is he single?" Dakota pushed the red curls back from her face as Manuel jostled toward us.

"Hey, can I sit with you guys? I was hoping to see you."

As Manuel set his tray down, Angie introduced him to the others.

"Hi!" Dakota flashed a smile. "Where you from?"

As Manuel ate his spaghetti, he told us that he'd moved from Dallas (the nearest big city to us), his parents were originally from Mexico, his mom had gotten a job as a math professor at the little college in our town, and his dad worked as a sales manager for some company.

I only half listened to what he said, paying more attention to his voice. It was soft and smooth, not gravelly like mine. I'd never liked my voice. And every time he looked at me, it was like *kapow!* Something happened inside me that I couldn't explain.

Then Elizabeth asked, "Are you a Christian?"

"Some days more than others." Manuel gave a relaxed grin. "But I try to be."

Elizabeth's brow knitted in confusion, and I was puzzled too. Either you were a Christian, meaning you accepted Jesus Christ as your Lord and savior, or you didn't and you weren't.

Angie and Dakota moved on to other new-friend questions: Manuel's favorite color? Purple. Favorite season? Spring. Favorite ice cream? Chocolate Chip Cookie Dough.

He asked us the same sort of stuff and then said, "Hey, does your school have a GSA?"

"A what?" Angie's nose crinkled with curiosity.

"A gay-straight alliance," Dakota interjected.

At the mention of the word "gay," I recalled the dream that had woken me that morning, and my face flamed.

"My cousin told me," Dakota continued, "that they started a GSA at her school in Houston. She said it caused a huge ruckus. Some churches even tried to stop it."

"Ugh!" Elizabeth paled in horror. "They'd never allow a group like *that* here."

"They barely even let us have dances," Angie complained.

"So . . ." Dakota, intrepid journalist and always to the point, leaned toward Manuel. "Are *you* gay?"

I expected him to laugh or get angry, but he calmly twirled his spaghetti noodles. "Yep."

Elizabeth's jaw dropped. Angie's eyes grew wide. And

my heart skipped a beat. He couldn't possibly mean it. Could he?

"Don't worry." Manuel glanced around at us, half grinning and half serious. "It's not contagious."

Dakota pealed with laughter, while the rest of us sat stunned. How could he joke like that? Didn't he realize the consequences of what he was saying? Students would shun and ridicule him—or worse. He *had* to be kidding.

"Are you serious?" Angie asked, and Manuel nodded.

Elizabeth braced herself on the table. "You mean you're a practicing homosexual?"

Manuel studied her a moment, as if debating whether to take her question seriously. "Well, actually, I think I've got the hang of it by now."

Elizabeth frowned, and Angie commented, "I don't think any of us have ever met anybody gay before."

Manuel gazed toward me. Quickly I averted my eyes. Why was he looking at *me*?

"But you can't be homosexual *and* Christian," Elizabeth sputtered. "That's impossible!"

"Well . . ." Manuel gave a casual shrug, although his voice sounded a little defensive. "What about John Three-Sixteen? Or did I overlook the fine print?"

In our little corner of the Bible Belt, it wasn't unusual for someone to cite the famous verse: *For God so loved the world that he gave his only Son, that whoever believes in him should not perish but have eternal life.* But I'd never heard anybody quote it to include someone gay. I'd been taught that gay or lesbian people had turned away from God.

As I glanced up at the girls, a million questions swirled in my mind. If Manuel truly was gay (which I still couldn't believe he'd actually admit), then why was he quoting Scripture? Had he ever actually read the Bible? Didn't he understand he was going to hell?

My friends and I stared across the table at one another, as if each expected one of the others to defuse the bomb of confusion that had landed in our midst. And inside myself, doubts and worries I'd fought off for years bombarded me.

Without anyone noticing, I slipped my hands beneath the lunch table and snapped my wristband against my wrist.

2

MY EARLIEST MEMORY

OF BECOMING A CHRISTIAN TAKES PLACE AT THE LITTLE
CHURCH MY MA JOINED WHEN MY FAMILY MOVED TO TEXAS.
One wall of my Sunday school classroom displayed a bright
life-size mural of Jesus draped in pristine robes. Handsome,
white-skinned, and blue-eyed, he sat surrounded by beaming
children from different nations. One boy wore a turban,
another a serape. A girl wore a kimono. Each child leaned forward as if listening raptly, while Jesus pointed toward the bil-
lowy clouds above him. Though the painting now sounds sort
of contrived, when I was a boy it impressed me vividly.

I sat in the front row, staring at the mural, while hearing
the passionate stories of Moses, David, St. Paul, and Jesus. I
wanted to be like them: brave, pure, and good. I wanted to
feel God's strength and love.

For my First Communion present, my ma gave me a
leather-bound Holy Bible. The rich, clean smell of glue and

fresh ink seeped into my lungs as I turned the crisp tissue-paper pages with their shining gold edges. I carefully ran my small hands across the words Jesus spoke (printed in red) and the multicolored maps of the Holy Land. So began my love for the book that would guide my life.

All through grade school I carried my Bible everywhere, memorizing whole chunks of Scripture, striving to show God how much I loved him. I'm not exactly sure why winning God's approval was so important to me, but it was.

Then, in middle school, my faith received a huge test: puberty. My health classes had prepared me for the biological consequences. My voice started to change and my first pubic fuzz appeared. But no one had forewarned me that the most noteworthy consequence for boys might pop up inside my pants at moments that totally mystified me. (Like at little league, when a teammate scratched his tightly uniformed thigh, or at Vacation Bible School, each time my suntanned youth minister leaned close and I smelled his musky cologne.) At home in my room I pondered my unwanted physical reactions and began to detect a worrisome pattern: They were all directed toward guys.

A sickening feeling gripped my stomach. Around that same time I had begun to hear in church that homosexuality was a sin and that "Sodomites" were destined to hell. I didn't want to sin, and I definitely didn't want to be condemned to hell. So why was I having these feelings?

At school one boy who the other guys said was "queer" got beaten up nearly every day. I watched and recalled the story of the Good Samaritan. I wanted to help him. But what if people began to think I was gay too? Instead I turned away.

I began to be on guard—even when asleep. Although my health texts had advised me to expect sex dreams, mine weren't about the opposite sex like those books said. In my dreams I was being hugged and kissed *by boys.*

I woke up in a sweat, confused and terrified. After fumbling for the light, I scrambled to my knees beside the bed. "Why am I feeling this way?" I asked God. "You know I don't want to. Why is this happening to me?"

I listened in silence, waiting for an answer. But none came.

Too ashamed to talk to anyone about it, I went back to my health books, desperate for hope. To my relief, I discovered two tiny sentences buried in a footnote:

During puberty some girls and boys may feel sexual curiosity toward others of the same sex. Such feelings are a temporary phase that will soon pass.

I drank from that promise like from some spring in a desert of doubt. And just as I'd tried to bury the fact that I was Mexican, I stuffed the possibility I might be gay into a box deep inside my heart.

To escape thinking about it, I involved myself big-time in sports, competing in swimming, track, and especially cross-country, going on long runs and praying with each step. I spoke openly to everyone about being a Christian. And to Angie I professed my love.

She and I had been pretty inseparable ever since my family had arrived from Mexico. At the time I didn't speak a word of English. The boys in class cracked up and made fun of me, but the girl beside me with the sleek black ponytail told them, "Shush!" and gently corrected my pronunciation.

I repeated the words she taught me over and over, determined to get them exactly right, till she'd finally tell me, "Take it easy! You're too hard on yourself." The guys teased me that I'd catch girl cooties, but I ignored them. Like Angie's name suggested, she was kind of an angel for me. By second grade I had progressed to the advanced reading group, stopped speaking Spanish altogether, and started going by Paul instead of Pablo.

Angie and I sat side by side at lunch, hung out at each other's homes after school, talked for hours on the phone, and IMed way past bedtime. In middle school, at a birthday party truth-or-dare game, Angie and I kissed for the first time. It was just a peck, really. But it made us officially boyfriend and girlfriend.

After that we walked hand in hand at the mall, went to

dances together, and gave each other gifts and heart-shaped cards. By high school, we were voted Cutest Couple, even though we never majorly made out—much less did anything approaching sex.

I never spoke to her about the confused feelings that troubled me, maybe because I feared talking about it would make it more real. I wasn't ready for that. And besides, how could I explain what was happening when I didn't understand it myself? Instead I prayed for God to change me and hoped that Angie wouldn't end up hurt. What if she did find out my secret thoughts?

On the outside, I was a model of all-American heterosexual Christian boyhood. (Being tall for my age no doubt helped.) But on the inside, I felt like a fraud, smaller than a bug.

What's life without a little . . .

DRAMA!

★ A new series by Paul Ruditis ★

At Bryan Stark's posh private high school in Malibu, the teens are entitled, the boys are cute, and the school musicals are *extremely* elaborate. Bryan watches—and comments—as the action and intrigue unfold around him. Thrilling mysteries, comic relief, and epic sagas of friendship and love . . . It's all here. And it's showtime.

From Simon Pulse • Published by Simon & Schuster

From bestselling author
KATE BRIAN

♥ ♥ ♥ ♥ ♥

Juicy reads for the sweet and the sassy!

Sweet 16
As seen in *CosmoGIRL!*

Lucky T
"Fans of Meg Cabot's *The Princess Diaries* will enjoy it." —*SLJ*

Megan Meade's Guide to the McGowan Boys
Featured in *Teen* magazine!

The Virginity Club
"*Sex and the City: High School Edition.*" —*KLIATT*

The Princess & the Pauper
"Truly exceptional chick-lit." —*Kirkus Reviews*

FROM SIMON PULSE
♥ Published by Simon & Schuster ♥